Fabulous Fathers

Adam looked from her to the child in his arms. "I still can't believe what you did."

His accusation shattered the reverence of the moment. "Well," Evie said, "I guess I'll just have to learn to live with that."

His eyes snapped toward her. "You'll be moving back into the house, then," he said. His words weren't a question, but rather a command.

"My plans haven't changed. I'll be taking the baby back with me."

His voice was quiet, but his words were edged in steel. "I don't think so. You're not taking my little girl away from me again."

Dear Reader,

What makes a man a Fabulous Father? For me, he's the man who married my single mother when she had three little kids (who all needed braces) and raised us as his own. And, to celebrate an upcoming anniversary of the Romance line's FABULOUS FATHERS series, I'd like to know *your* thoughts on what makes a man a Fabulous Father. Send me a brief (50 words) note with your name, city and state, giving me permission to publish all or portions of your note, and you just might see it printed on a special page.

Blessed with a baby—and a second chance at marriage—this month's FABULOUS FATHER also has to become a fabulous husband to his estranged wife in *Introducing Daddy* by Alaina Hawthorne.

"Will you marry me, in name only?" That's a woman's desperate question to the last of THE BEST MEN, Karen Rose Smith's miniseries, in *A Groom and a Promise*.

He drops her like a hot potato, then comes back with babies and wants her to be his nanny! Or so he says…in *Babies and a Blue-Eyed Man* by Myrna Mackenzie.

When a man has no memory and a woman needs an instant husband, she tells him a little white lie and presto! in *My Favorite Husband* by Sally Carleen.

She's a waitress who needs etiquette lessons in becoming a lady; he's a millionaire who likes her just the way she is in *Wife in Training* by Susan Meier.

Finally, Robin Wells is one of Silhouette's WOMEN TO WATCH—a new author debuting in the Romance line with *The Wedding Kiss*.

I hope you enjoy all our books this month—and every month!

Regards,

Melissa Senate,
Senior Editor

Please address questions and book requests to:
Silhouette Reader Service
U.S.: 3010 Walden Ave., P.O. Box 1325, Buffalo, NY 14269
Canadian: P.O. Box 609, Fort Erie, Ont. L2A 5X3

INTRODUCING DADDY

Alaina Hawthorne

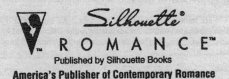

Silhouette®

R O M A N C E™

Published by Silhouette Books

America's Publisher of Contemporary Romance

As always, eternal thanks to Pat Kay,
Heather MacAllister, Marilyn Amann and Carla Luan.

For Julian Staehely.

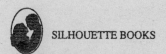 SILHOUETTE BOOKS

ISBN 0-373-19180-4

INTRODUCING DADDY

Copyright © 1996 by Alaina W. Richardson

This edition published by arrangement with Harlequin Books S.A.

Printed in U.S.A.

Books by Alaina Hawthorne

Silhouette Romance

Out of the Blue #672
The Bridal Path #1029
My Dearly Beloved #1069
Make-Believe Bride #1164
Introducing Daddy #1180

ALAINA HAWTHORNE,

a native Texan, has been writing fiction and nonfiction since she was a teenager. Her first Silhouette Romance won the Romance Writers of America's RITA Award for Best First Book. She lives in Houston with Sallie, her rottweiler, and loves hearing from her readers. Write to Alaina at P.O. Box 820342, Houston, TX 77282.

Adam Rabalais On Fatherhood:

Dear Juliette,

Words cannot express how much joy you have brought into my life. I didn't realize that working eighty hours a week meant nothing without someone to come home to. And now that you and your mother are back in my life, I vow to become the perfect daddy.

I've been reading up on fatherhood, little girl, catching up on those months I missed. I'm so sorry I didn't get to hold you right after you were born, or that I wasn't there for your first smile. But I do promise to be there for your first word, your first step. We'll go for walks in the park. I'll come to all of your ballet recitals. Together we'll be the best father-and-daughter team around.

Remember, you are the most precious gift I've ever received.

All my love,

Daddy

Chapter One

Sheets of rain sluiced against the windows of the shop, and every so often thunder boomed in the distance and rattled the panes. Through the gray rivulets Evie Rabalais could just make out the waists of Houston's skyscrapers; the tops of the buildings were plunged into the clouds that had hovered over the city for days. The radio said the bayous were jumping their banks. Beneath the streets the storm drains roared with brown foamy water. Evie stood by the front door, arms crossed and motionless, and watched the traffic—wheel-deep in water—crawl miserably down Westheimer. Her mood matched the bleak weather.

Edward and Frank, both of the part-time delivery drivers, had called in saying they couldn't make it into the shop because of the flooding. Evie wondered if that was really true. She scowled and sighed. Not that their absence would make much difference. This type of weather was terrible for business. There wouldn't be any foot traffic at all today, and gloomy weather also seemed to affect human generosity: there were always fewer orders when it rained.

When the phone suddenly jangled, Evie flinched and crossed quickly to the desk. She wanted to catch it before the ringing woke Juliette. The baby had fussed all night. Since it was too soon for her to be teething, Evie assumed the infant had sensed her unhappiness and responded to it. All the books she'd read said babies were sensitive to moods.

She lifted the receiver. "Something Different. This is Evie, may I help you?"

"Um, yes, I think—well, I hope so."

The woman's voice was high-pitched and tentative. A nervous type, Evie thought. This might take a while.

"Um, are you that place that makes those gift baskets with all kinds of, you know, different stuff?"

"Yes, ma'am," Evie replied. "We make gift baskets and boxes for all occasions. Our slogan is Why Just Send Something When You Can Send 'Something Different.'" Evie winced. It sounded stupid today. But then, she thought, it could just be the way she was feeling.

"Oh, good. Let's see, well, I'm not really sure what I want. I mean this may not be appropriate. I . . . well, it's—you see, there was a picture in yesterday's paper. A business associate of my husband's. The caption was about some sort of charity thingie . . ."

Ah, of course, a charity thingie.

"...but the caption hinted that she might be getting engaged, too."

Getting engaged, too? Surely it can't be... Evie choked, but the woman apparently didn't hear her.

"It's not for sure, you see, so I don't really know if it's appropriate to send, you know, congratulations. The paper implied it was just a rumor, you know, but Betsy's never wrong. She knows everyone and everything. Like God." The woman cackled at her own joke. Evie wrestled with the urge to slam down the phone and run from the room.

"Anyway, so Vic, my husband, he wants to be the first to send something if there really is an engagement. Nothing too obvious or flashy, you know. Kind of a two-way gift—mostly for the award, but with something about the engagement, too. Something in the two-hundred-and-fifty range. What do you think?"

I think I'm going to start screaming. For one panic-stricken instant Evie considered saying that they were closed—going out of business even. She didn't want to scour her favorite shops and bookstores for beautiful, thoughtful gifts. But the woman had said "the two-hundred-and-fifty range." The shop had suffered over the past week. Olivia would be thrilled to hear someone wanted to spend more than two hundred dollars. Evie swallowed and tried to sound normal. "Do you know any of her interests? If you give us a couple of days I'm sure I can—"

The woman gave a little scream of protest. "Oh, no, no, no. It has to be delivered today. Before noon, in fact. You can do that, can't you?"

Evie swallowed hard. It wasn't so much that she had to make a suitable presentation from the available inventory—there were plenty of beautiful things in the shop. But there would be no one to deliver the basket. Except her.

"I see. Yes, of course, we can do that. Well, how about a nice Burka hamper with a book of poems and...champagne and flutes. We can also enclose a gift certificate for a day-long session at La Paradise..." For what seemed an eternity, Evie made tasteful suggestions, understated suggestions. No matter how outraged and betrayed she felt, she knew she would have to choke back her anger. The basket would be elegant; nothing ostentatious or overwhelming. She was very good at her job.

Her client clucked and exclaimed gleefully over each recommendation, and in less than twenty minutes every item had been approved.

"Thank you so much, Edie," the woman gushed. "I know she's going to love it—"

"It's Evie."

"And you'll guarantee she'll have it before noon. We don't want anyone to beat us to the punch. Oh, and the card will have to say congratulations or something. Only not the word *congratulations*. I think that's too masculine, don't you? And you should see her, she's such a gorgeous girl. I just hate her." The woman hooted at her own humor. "Now, it's for Kimberley Van Kyle at Van Kyle Oil. Van Kyle is two words, capital *V* and capital *K*."

"Yes, I know."

Evie had also read the item in the Sunday Metropolitan section of the paper. "Kimberley Van Kyle Receives Nighthawk Award." Besides, Evie had known how to spell the name Van Kyle for years. After all, Van Kyle Oil had been instrumental in the disintegration of her marriage. She'd even met Kimberley three or four years ago at a Christmas party at the Van Kyles' River Oaks estate.

That was long ago. Yesterday's paper was the first time Evie had thought of Elvin Van Kyle's daughter in years. Olivia had seen the article, too. She'd stayed up with Evie well past midnight listening to her cry and rail against the beautiful heiress and her ruggedly handsome companion. In the photograph, just to the right and behind the stunning redhead stood Kimberley's escort for the charity gala, Adam Rabalais. Evie hadn't even known he was back in the country. She recalled the almost physically sickening sensation of seeing the photograph—the exuberant, smiling faces. She had stared at the picture with the same fascinated horror a patient regards a terminal X ray. She had no idea how many times she'd read Betsy's chatty tidbit.

And who's the tall, silent hunk escorting Kimmie? Mizz Van K's not spilling any beans, but folks in the know have mentioned wedding bells...

Evie jerked herself back to the present and tried to concentrate on her customer's voice. She repeated the address, which she already knew. Van Kyle Oil occupied six floors in One Shell Plaza, smack in the middle of downtown Houston. Evie nearly shuddered. She hated downtown.

"And you will guarantee the basket arrives before lunch?" The woman now sounded peevish.

"Yes," Evie replied quietly. "Before lunch. I'll take care of it myself."

Evie set the receiver quietly in the cradle. Why, she wondered, why, of all the places in Houston to call would she have to call us? It was probably the advertising, Evie reasoned, not some cruel twist of fate. Lately Olivia had taken out a couple of ads in the downtown tabloids and shoppers' guides. Evie dropped her forehead on her arms and let a few hot tears slip out.

She willed herself not to cry anymore. It was so odd, she almost never cried, but last night she'd boo-hooed so hard her face was as swollen as if she'd stuck it in a beehive. This morning her puffy, reddened eyes defied her attempts to camouflage them with makeup. She eventually gave up and washed the mess off. Or most of it.

Rings of stubborn mascara still circled her eyelids, since the baby's hungry demands had superseded her attempts to scrub it away. Besides, she hadn't planned on leaving the shop all day. No one here gave a damn if she looked like a raccoon.

But now she was going to have to go downtown. What if she had to come face-to-face with Kimberley? With Adam? She took a calming breath. That would never happen. She wouldn't go near the executive floors. She'd make up the basket, hustle downtown and drop it off with the receptionist. No fuss, no muss. In and out. After all, she'd done it a hundred times in buildings all over the city. But despite her efforts to be brave, Evie felt a deepening of the pain in her torso.

This is why they call it a heartache—it really hurts. I can't stand this feeling. How long does it last? Months? Years?

She bit her lip. Maybe Olivia could make the...but no, Olivia never made deliveries. After all, she owned the shop, and besides, she was past seventy and too frail to wrestle with the cantankerous transmission of the van or lug around heavy gift baskets. Evie glanced up at the clock. Nine forty-five. She mentally calculated the amount of time it would take to fill the order. An hour to put the basket together. Twenty minutes to make it downtown in the rain. Another fifteen to park and get up to the thirtieth floor. If she got right to work she'd make it just in time.

Twenty minutes later Olivia came down the stairs from her apartment over the shop. Evie's quarters took up the back half of the top floor of the giant old Victorian house.

"Is that an order?" she asked, obviously pleased.

Evie nodded, but couldn't hold her friend's gaze for long. The minute she saw sympathy in those warm, gentle eyes, she knew she would start crying again. Still, there was no hiding her feelings from Olivia.

"What is it, honey? Are you still...?"

Evie shrugged and gestured toward the order pad.

"Two hundred and fifty dollars?" Olivia exclaimed. "But why the long face? This is wonderful. Praise the— Oh. Oh, dear. I...what did you say?"

"What could I say? I promised to have it there before noon as requested."

"Evie, I'm sorry. Call her back. Tell her we can't—"

"No way. We need the order. It's been a crummy week."

Olivia opened her mouth to protest but slowly closed it. The shop hung on by a tenuous thread at the best of times. "Maybe I could take it."

Evie rolled her eyes. "Thanks for offering, 'Liv, but downtown's horrible even when you know your way around." She sighed. "Besides, this thing's gonna weigh a ton. Would you look at the size of it? You'd be doubled over for a week."

Frown lines creased the older woman's forehead. "I'm going to murder Ed and Frankie. If I find out they're somewhere goofing off I'll..."

Evie gave her friend an attempt at a smile. "Oh, well, we were young once, too. I used to love to goof off on gloomy days, didn't you? Hot chocolate, good books or an old movie. Maybe even a fire. Or best of all..." Evie's voice was beginning to shake.

Adam had loved rainy days. Years ago when they were first married, he'd worked construction to put himself through grad school, but every rainy day meant the work stopped. Back then Adam always seemed gleeful to have a day alone with her.

"I arranged this for us," he'd say. "I just used my magic words— Come on, rain clouds, show your power. Adam wants a shutdown shower."

He was greedy for her in those days. If it was winter they'd build a fire, and if it was summer they would fill the fireplace with candles and enjoy the colors of the little flames dancing on smooth skin. Adam almost always insisted that they splurge on a bottle of good wine, and they'd take turns reading passages of their favorite books to each other.

After love, it was always the same. He would trace slow patterns on her back. "Guess what I'm writing," he'd say. "Now, if you win…" Most of the time they skipped dinner and fell asleep curved together on the hearth.

But those times were gone—eroded by years of explosive arguments, hurt silences and the slow, creeping abandonment of two people sharing less and less. Sometimes Evic still couldn't comprehend exactly what had happened.

"I'll make us some tea." Olivia said softly. She had heard most of Evie's story over the past ten months. The rest she just seemed to understand without being told.

Before she left, she paused to look at the artfully packed basket to which Evie was just applying a few special touches—sheer pastel cellophane and satin ribbons. "Beautiful work as always. Are you sure you can do this?"

"Oh, it won't be so bad. I'll just put on Frank's slicker, pull the hood over my head and duck behind this big thing." She smiled. "Besides, there's nothing to worry about. There's no way I'll run into either of them."

By the time Evie pulled into the underground loading area beneath One Shell Plaza, her nerves were even more frayed than before. Just as she'd been leaving the shop, Juliette had woken up squalling and had refused to settle down. Not even Olivia had been able to do anything to soothe her. Then Westheimer had been flooded at three intersections, and though the van rode high, other cars had stalled and traffic had backed up for blocks.

Finally she'd had to circle around and take the Allen Parkway. The trip that normally took twenty minutes had taken almost three-quarters of an hour. By the time Evie had turned onto Louisiana Street she'd felt the beginnings of a potent and long-lasting headache. Traffic had been snarled around the building, and she'd had to spend another fifteen minutes inching toward the light at the corner of Walker. When she'd finally made the turn into the underground parking, there hadn't been a single space in the loading dock.

Evie checked her watch. Fifteen minutes until twelve. The tunnel system would be crowded with lunch traffic—dry, smartly dressed, professional people. Evie was soaked just from walking from the shop to the van. Wind had blown the rain almost horizontally. Her hair, which normally fell in bouncy natural ringlets past her shoulders was wildly corkscrewed and unruly from the humidity.

She double-parked next to a courier's truck and stepped out of the driver's side into an inch and a half of water. As the brackish runoff soaked into her good running shoes, Evie indulged her temper with a few words she seldom used and went to the back of the van. It took both arms to carry the basket, and she had to peek around it to see where she was going.

She stopped at the security window and balanced the basket against the narrow ledge to sign in.

"Where'd you park?" the attendant asked, not looking up.

"I'm doubled, but there's plenty of room for the other guy to get around me."

"Can't do that, lady. You'll get towed."

Evie felt the ache in her chest ratchet up a notch. "But there's nowhere else. I'm running late and I'll only be five minutes. I'm just going up to Van Kyle to deliver this."

He glanced up with unsympathetic hazel eyes. "Suit yourself," he said. "But if you're not down in fifteen minutes, it'll be towed."

Evie scrawled her signature and bumped the heavy swinging door open with her hip. The blast of air-conditioning made her damp skin feel clammy, and the distant murmur of voices echoing through the tunnels sounded spooky and disquieting.

As soon as she passed through the double swinging doors of the service entrance she saw the sea of bodies surging through the narrow underground walkways. She wasn't really surprised at the crush of people; no one would brave the weather outside today unless it was an absolute necessity.

The knot of people waiting at the tunnel level elevator was at least twenty deep, so she made a quick decision and took an escalator up to the street level. Through the glass walls of the lobby Evie could see City Hall and the dark green oaks that lined the reflection pool. Their crowns whipped in the stiff breeze while the fractured surface of the pool reflected the dark underbelly of the sky.

Across the street the fountains in Tranquility Park gushed water straight up, where the wind immediately tore it away while simultaneously dumping rain back down into the stone-lined ponds. Evie glanced back at City Hall clock. The day was so dark the hands glowed red even at noon. High noon. She was now officially late.

The lobby was choked with people pressed almost up to the glass, some waiting to bolt for cabs as they pulled up on Smith Street, some just eager to leave their desks but not wanting to brave the tunnels or venture far in the wretched weather. A few miserable smokers huddled outside against flanks of the building, obviously unable to wait until after work to indulge in their cigarettes.

Evie thought the people looked as gray and threatening as the sky. The women wore dark power suits, chopped-off hair and sculpted nails, and the men glided among them as smoothly and gracefully as sharks. At least it seemed that way to her.

She shrugged her yellow slicker a little higher on her shoulders and hefted up the basket. On both sides of her face, her wiry hair seemed to be trying to claw its way out of the hood by itself. More than anything Evie wanted to put the damn basket down and shove the ugly mess back under her hood, but there was nowhere to stop.

The One Shell Plaza lobby was a gleaming expanse of white, echoing marble with polished brass appointments and ruthlessly tamed ficus trees standing obediently erect in their architectural planters. The seating edge of the planters didn't look inviting at all. In fact, Evie wouldn't dare sit down on one. She had a feeling that there was a ficus guard lurking somewhere who'd leap out, grab her by her collar and make a humiliating example of her in front of all the frosty-eyed MBAs and their administrative assistants. No, she thought, best to just hurry up and get this over with as soon as possible.

When the elevator doors closest to her slid open, she practically lunged in. She ignored the disapproving looks and noises from the people she'd shoved past, but this was an emergency. Besides, she told herself, the predatory downtown atmosphere was contagious; here it was every man for himself. God, if she didn't hurry up and get out of here she'd turn into one of them.

She elbowed the button for the thirty-eighth floor and then pressed herself to the back of the car. In the close quiet of the little space she became aware of noises she hadn't noticed earlier—the crackle of the cellophane, the squishy noise of her soaked sneakers and the cheap rustle of her yellow slicker. She felt a slight itch, just a tickle really, just alongside her nose.

Somewhere between the thirty-first and thirty-third floors a particularly loud and long roll of thunder rumbled outside. The lights flickered and the elevator car hesitated. One of the passengers groaned.

"Not again."

"Did you hear? Melvin got stuck in the elevator for an hour on Saturday."

"I'd lose it."

"We could have taken the stairs."

"Are you nuts? Forty-some-odd floors?"

While the others swapped elevator war stories, Evie kept her head ducked and counted the minutes. Every time the car stopped passengers changed; some got off, some on. She pressed herself as deeply into her corner as she could and tried not to see the people, not to hear them. She wished she could look at her watch. Had it been fifteen minutes? Did the security guard really mean he'd *have* the van towed in fifteen minutes or he'd *call* to have it towed in fifteen minutes?

Again the car stopped and this time the elevator disgorged nearly all its passengers. Before the doors closed two men stepped on—charcoal gray legs and khaki legs. Khaki Legs said, "So, are we on for Wednesday?"

"Wednesday's good for me."

That's all he said. Just "Wednesday's good for me," but Evie's body underwent the same reaction it had the first time she'd heard that voice fourteen years earlier. The hair on her nape stood, and her stomach erupted in a storm of butterflies.

Oh, please, no. Don't let him see me. Please. I'll go to Mass, to confession even. I'll make the nine first Fridays. I'll join the Altar Society. Hail, Mary, full of grace—

Another boom of thunder seemed to make the whole building shudder, and the lights flicked off for a full three seconds.

"That was close," Adam Rabalais murmured. "Think it struck the building?"

"Could have," his companion answered. "Happens all the time."

Evie held her breath. *I'll stay on until he gets off. I don't care if I have to ride this thing to the moon.*

Something told her he was looking at her, noticing her. But how could he not be curious? There were only three of them in the elevator—two smartly dressed businessmen and one extremely short person who wore squishy sneakers, rumpled, rain-soaked jeans and carried an enormous Burmese hamper. That same person was obviously cowering under an old, yellow rain slicker and had frantic blue-black ringlets of hair crawling out of her hood.

Why? she wondered. Why is this happening? It's like a nightmare or a horrible movie. Evie bowed her head against the basket. The cellophane crackled maliciously.

When the elevator car creaked to a stop Khaki Legs exited. "I'll call you Wednesday when I'm on my way," he said.

"Right. Wednesday, then," Adam replied. Evie recognized the thoughtful tone in his voice.

She felt bereft. She almost wanted to follow dear old Khaki Legs out but she had no idea what floor they were on. She didn't dare to look up to check, either. Besides, if she started to get off, Adam would notice that there was still another floor punched. He might speak to her, and if she answered, he'd recognize her voice for sure. And her height. She was so damned short.

Why didn't I wear tall shoes, she wondered. Oh, right . . . wet blue jeans and pumps. Just what all the delivery drivers are wearing. What could possibly be more low profile? Please, God, she prayed, please don't let him talk to me.

"That's a beautiful basket, but it's nearly as big as you are."

You just have to be Mr. Friendly, don't you? Why can't you leave me alone? "Mmmm," she answered, trying to disguise her voice and ducking her head even lower. She wished she could hide her bony little hands and the frenzied hair that refused to stay wadded up inside her hood.

A moment of cold, pregnant silence ensued, during which Evie sent up one more desperate prayer that Adam hadn't recognized her voice—that he wouldn't try to make her say anything else and give herself away completely. She swallowed and kept her gaze riveted to the floor. The angle of his gleaming wingtips told her that he'd turned to face her.

"Who's it for?"

Oh, God, he knows. Evie didn't answer.

"I said, who's it for?" This time his voice was peremptory and demanding.

Evie looked up hot-faced and unashamed of the sheen in her eyes. "Your fiancée, Adam."

For a fleeting instant a look of joyful disbelief flashed across his face, and he stepped toward her—almost reflexively. Then his look hardened.

Evie took a deep breath to make sure her voice was steady. "By the way, when were you planning to tell her that you're still married to me?"

Chapter Two

Evie's heart slammed in her chest as Adam nailed her with a cold glare.

"I'm surprised to hear you ask that, Evie. Since when do you care where I go or who I spend time with?"

She glared right back into his eyes. The first time Mrs. Alexander had seen him, she'd remarked, "Gray as rain. Even when he laughs he looks so sad. His eyes are the color of tears."

Evie raised her chin and tried to make her face hard. "I *don't* care," she said. "I'd just find it a little embarrassing to be married to a bigamist."

"Well," he said, "thanks so much for your overwhelming warmth and concern."

Evie scowled at him, then faced the door. The elevator shuddered, and a deep, faraway rumble told her the storm still churned overhead. *I'm not going to look at him. Maybe this isn't happening. Maybe I'm having a horrible nightmare.*

She could feel him staring at her. Waves of hostile incredulity poured through the tiny space. How long had it been since she'd seen him? Nine months? No, ten. And how long before that had it been since they'd looked at each other with anything other than anger and resentment?

The last time she'd spoken to him was more than six months ago when he'd called from Buenos Aires and caught her at her aunt's house, but that conversation hadn't lasted long. As usual, it took only moments before one of them started yelling and the other one slammed down the phone. That last conversation had ended on a particularly devastating note. And now, here she was, suspended with him in an eight-by-eight-foot box somewhere halfway up One Shell Plaza.

When thunder boomed again, the car hesitated and the lights flickered. Evie groaned against the feeling of weightless nausea and hugged her basket tighter. *No, not this. Not now.* Once again they began to rise, but in only seconds, with a hydraulic scream, the elevator car bounced to a stop. Evie heard her breath escaping with a terrified hiss; Adam didn't even seem to notice they'd quit moving.

He uncrossed his arms but didn't step toward her, he just rocked forward on the balls of his feet. "I'm sorry, Evie. That's not what I meant to say."

She cut him the ugliest glance she could manage and then turned away again. The pressure of furious tears intensified in the back of her throat. *Hurry, elevator.*

Hurry, hurry. She clutched the hamper to her middle and hoped that the huge basket would disguise her weight loss, her pale complexion and her brimming, swollen eyes. *I won't look at him, and that way I won't cry. And I don't have to say anything, either. I'll just deliver my basket and get the hell out of here, and things will go on just like I planned.* "What's wrong with this thing? Is there a phone in here?" What she wanted to do was scream, *Let me out.*

"It's okay," Adam said quietly. "We'll start up again in a minute. This happens a lot."

For a moment he was quiet, but she felt him looking at her. "I've been trying to get in touch with you for months," he said. "Nobody will give me your number."

"Good." Her voice was definitely wobbling. God, she hated that. And why did she have to look like something the cat wouldn't even bother to drag in? Not that it mattered. In fact, this was probably better. Adam, of course, looked impeccable in perfectly tailored Savile Row. Evie recognized the suit from one of his trips to the U.K. Last year? No, two years ago. She remembered because he'd been gone for their anniversary. And her birthday.

"Why, Evie? Why won't you even talk to me?"

She didn't look at him. "What's the use? What could we say that we haven't already said a thousand times?"

"I may have said it a thousand times, but it's still true. I want you to come home, Evie."

There was no avoiding it, she had to look at him; talking at the elevator doors was stupid. She sighed.

"And where's home this week? Argentina? Outer Mongolia? And how would you even know if I were home or not? *You* hardly ever bothered to show up there." She took a quick breath and her voice lowered. "Half the time I didn't even know where you were unless your secretary told me. I didn't know you were back in the country until I saw your *engagement notice* in the paper."

He winced. "Damn. I *knew* you'd see that piece of bull—but it wasn't an engagement notice. Kimberley and I just went to a company function together because she didn't have a date." He paused for a long moment. "And I had no idea how to get in touch with my *wife*."

His voice had been growing hard, but then his tone softened. "That was just stupid gossip from a stupid gossip column, you know that. Besides, you know Kimberley. She's just a kid."

"We're the same age."

He shook his head slightly. "For Pete's sake, Evie, I've known her since she started college, and—"

"You've known me since I was in junior high."

Adam's mouth closed in a hard line, and with the deepest satisfaction Evie saw that he was losing his temper—that she'd gotten to him. Good, she thought. In the past she had never won any arguments. Adam could always talk circles around her. No matter how prepared she thought she was, she would always wind up ranting or crying, while Adam maintained his maddeningly unflappable calm.

"The point is, Evangeline," he said slowly, "that I want you with me. I always have."

"No, Adam," she countered, "you don't want me with you. You want someone at home in case you decide to show up there. You want dinner on the table and your errands run. You want an acceptable arm hanger for social functions and someone to see that your family gets Christmas cards and birthday presents."

"Evie, please, not this again."

"You started it."

When she saw the flash of hopelessness cross his face she turned away. Despite everything that had happened between them, she still hated to see him unhappy. *Be strong. You know what's at stake here. If he knew...*

"Couldn't we go somewhere and just talk?"

The ache in his voice wrenched her heart. Part of her—most of her—wanted more than anything to spend hours, years, talking to him. Any second she knew she might drop the basket along with the pretense of anger and fling herself into his arms. *Yes, right back into the same situation you were in for the past seven years. But it's not just the two of you anymore, is it? Think of her.* That one thought evaporated her momentary fantasy of a tearful reconciliation.

She looked straight into his gray eyes. *You'd better make this convincing.* "You don't get it, do you?" The shock and pain in his face twisted her insides. "Remember the last time that I said 'This is the last time?' Well, believe it or not, it really was the very last time." Her voice was thinning out, and she felt the return of incipient tears. "I think it's pretty obvious—

it's been obvious for years—that we want different things, Adam. Different lives.''

"I don't,'' he said. "I want the life we had together back.''

"Well, excuse me,'' she said in a choked voice. "Maybe you want the same old life, but it's just not good enough for me anymore. I don't want to live alone. I want a husband and a family. I'm not a talking doll, Adam. Just once I'd like to come first—not second or third or fourth behind business meetings and rig workovers and power dinners—''

"You are the most important thing in the world to me, Evie. You always have been.''

"Am I? What about Christmas, Adam? What about the robbery? You left me to go off on your trip.''

Although it had almost been a year, the hideous images remained fresh in her mind—the drizzling December day, her back seat loaded with packages, carols on the radio as she'd stopped for the traffic light. The impact from the car slamming into her from behind had thrown her into the steering wheel and knocked her breath away. She hadn't known not to get out; she'd never even heard the expression "bump and rob.'' Besides, when she'd seen the sleek, luxury sedan behind her, it had never occurred to her that it might have been stolen.

By the time she'd opened her door, they'd already swarmed out of their car and had been waiting to jerk her off her feet and throw her down onto the concrete. The opening at the end of gun had looked enormous—like a black, toothless mouth. *Please, God,* she'd prayed. *Don't let him...*

"I made a mistake, Evie. But what was I supposed to do? The robbery was terrifying, I'll admit, but you weren't hurt, and the summit in Mexico was critical. You knew it meant jobs for hundreds of people, and I was the only one who... How many times do I have to say I'm sorry?"

But he hadn't been sorry at the time. His office had caught him at the airport that day, and he'd burst through the doors of the Emergency Room, wild-eyed with rage. But he hadn't canceled his business trip; he'd just put it off for a day.

One whole day.

She'd begged him not to leave. He'd begged her instead to come along with him—the negotiations were unraveling, he'd said. Governments were squaring off and a multinational consortium was on the verge of collapse.

Evie had raised her hands and showed him where the gravel had gouged away the skin. Then she'd pulled up her skirt to reveal the purple bruise on her thigh where one of them had stepped on her.

Still, he'd left the next day.

So had she.

That memory renewed her strength. "Well, here we go again," she said acidly. "you've started with Plan A and since that wasn't working you jumped directly to Plan C."

"What? Plan A? What—?"

"You see, Adam, over the past ten months I've had some time to figure things out. Whenever you don't show up or do what you promised, you always do one of three things. Plan A is you deny it. Plan B is you say something like, 'Okay, maybe I did do that, but it wasn't so bad.' If it's Plan C you say, 'Yeah, I did that and it was awful, but I'll never do it again.' But nothing changes. You always do exactly what you want no matter what you promised.''

The surge of angry strength was quickly spent, and when Evie went on, her voice was almost lost even in that small, quiet space. ''You send some little gift—or some big gift—and expect it to make up for any betrayal, any broken promise. But flowers aren't the same as a phone call, and a new bracelet isn't the same thing as coming home when you say you will. Material things don't equal time. Or love.''

Even though she spoke quietly, her words had their own power. ''If you loved me so much, why didn't I ever come first? Why wasn't I ever number one on your list of things to do? Or even number two? Or three? Our marriage was always the very last thing on your list of things to take care of.''

''Evie, you know how—''

The elevator suddenly lurched, and Evie let out a little scream.

''What the hell . . . ?'' Adam muttered.

''It's moving. Thank God.''

In seconds they stopped at the thirty-eighth floor, and the doors slid open. Evie stepped forward, sick with relief to make her escape. When Adam followed her, she stopped so fast he almost ran into her. ''This isn't your floor,'' she said.

He almost snorted. "You don't really think I'm just going to let you walk away, do you?"

She knew arguing was pointless, so she turned and stalked across the elevator lobby toward the glass doors. Adam's long strides easily carried him past her, and before she reached the door, he stepped in front and grabbed the brass pull.

"Thanks," she snapped.

"My pleasure."

The receptionist's desk sat on an emerald island of plush carpet set in the middle of a vast, marble floor and was flanked by deep leather couches and coffee tables. Behind her, a wall of glass looked north and west over the roofs of the Central Library and City Hall and beyond that to Allen's Landing and the tangled interchange of Interstate 45 and the Katy Freeway. The heavy sky roiled and glowered behind her.

At the sound of approaching footsteps, the stylishly gaunt young woman glanced up. Beneath the curving desk Evie could see that smoke-colored hose covered her shapely legs, and she wore forties-style shoes that revealed scarlet toenails. She gave Evie an assessing once-over, and her eyes registered cool disapproval, but when she saw Adam, her face broke into a radiant, porcelain-veneered smile. "Mr. Rabalais," she gushed.

"Hello, Lisa."

She beamed. "It's so nice to see you."

The girl's voice had risen and stretched out melodiously as she spoke to Adam. "So nice to see-e-e you." Oh, barf, Evie thought, and stomped across the floor so her shoes would really squish. She stopped in front of the desk and set the basket down. A leather desk blotter, a magazine and a nail file were arranged artfully next to a small phone set, and a computer sat blank and silent on one corner of the desk. Untouched by human hands, Evie thought, judging by the blonde's flawless manicure. "I have a delivery for Miss Van Kyle. Would you sign, please."

With obvious reluctance the girl tore her enraptured gaze from Adam's face and looked at Evie. "Of course," she said, and held out her hand. Her eyes immediately snapped back to their original target. "Is there someone I should buzz for you, Mr. Rabalais?"

"No, but thanks, Lisa. By the way, this is my wife, Evangeline. Evie, this is Lisa Roark."

The girl's eyes grew to the size of saucers, and she blushed very prettily and murmured something that sounded like, "It's very nice to... I-I'm sorry I didn't realize..."

Evie crimped her mouth into a smile. "Delighted," she said, and again glared at her husband. When the girl finished signing, Evie tore off the receipt, thanked her and turned. Adam's movements mirrored hers. Neither spoke until they stepped back into the elevator.

"Thank you for that, Adam."

"Delighted," he replied.

She felt him standing just behind her, his gaze boring a hole into her back. Her heart began to pound again and she stared at the ceiling, the door, the back of her left hand. When the doors opened, she practically leapt out. Obviously he planned to follow her to the garage. "What *are* you doing?" she flung at him over her shoulder. "You can't follow me. I'll start screaming. I'll make a scene, Adam, I mean it."

"Scream away. I told you before, Evie. I'm not letting you out of my sight until we talk."

She kept walking, then she stiff-armed the swinging doors to the loading dock and all but ran down the short hallway. "Lots of luck," she said. "You're gonna look pretty silly running behind the van."

He didn't answer.

The instant she reached the loading dock steps, her heart sank. She looked left. Right. Left again.

No van. "Oh, no."

"What is it?"

Evie ignored him and walked to the security window. "My van..."

The guard barely glanced up. "I told you, lady. Fifteen minutes."

Evie's chest tightened. "Thanks a lot. Now what do I do?"

He tapped the window with his pencil, and Evie saw the notice. For Towed Vehicles Call...

Oh, great. How much is this going to cost?

"Do you need a ride?"

"No, thank you. I'll get a cab." As soon as the words were out, Evie had a sickening realization. *And pay for it with what?* Her purse was carefully stowed under the front seat of the van. Besides, she couldn't afford cab rides. Even short ones. And how much was it going to cost to get the van out of storage? She could call Olivia, but then who would watch the baby?

Evie wanted to cry. She'd been gone three times longer than she'd intended—almost an hour and a half. It was time to feed Juliette. The van was gone. Her purse was gone. She had no money. And worst of all, Adam would now know where she worked. All he had to do was read the name on the delivery receipt. Since her apartment was over the shop, he'd know where she lived, too. He'd said he wasn't going to let her out of his sight until they talked, and she knew he meant it. She'd had plenty of experience with his stubborn streak over the years.

This had to happen sooner or later. Before you get on with your life you have things to settle with him. Now's as good a time as any. But Evie knew there would never be a good time to do what she knew she had to do. She'd put it off for months, but now events had overtaken her. Maybe it's best, she thought.

He was bound to find us someday.

Her shoulders slumped. Apparently Adam recognized the disintegration of her resolve. "Come with me," he urged. "I'm parked on the first level. You know I'll be glad to take you back to work."

Evie sighed. "Lead the way."

She turned to follow him. Mercifully, he kept all evidence of satisfaction out of his expression and just acted like anyone coming to the rescue of a stranded friend.

His car, as usual, was impressive—brand new with all the bells and whistles. Adam always did drive the best. She felt a momentary twinge about plopping her soaking wet bottom down on his plush seats, but there were so many other things to be miserable about, damp upholstery hardly rated a second thought.

For a moment she considered taking off the slicker and dropping it on the floorboard, but then he'd be sure to notice how much weight she'd lost. Instead, she just yanked the hood back. Her hair, freed at last, rose around her face like a curly, black sunburst. The bun wadded at the back of her neck immediately began to tickle in a really irritating way.

"Where are we going?" he asked.

So composed, she thought, so smooth—just like this is the most natural thing in the world. "The name of the shop is Something Different. It's on—"

"Westheimer. I've seen it." He turned the key, and the engine roused with a smug purr. Evie huddled against the door. Here she was, not two feet away from him. After all these months. After...everything else. She felt as if time had telescoped, as if the months had evaporated and they hadn't been separated at all.

You'd better tell him before we get to the shop. You know he's going to come in—if not today, someday soon. At the thought of it her stomach closed on itself and she clamped her arms over her middle.

"Are you all right?"

"Fine."

They ascended the ramp, and a sheet of rain smacked the windshield as the car emerged into the gray afternoon. Evie became aware of music on the stereo and recognized the song. "Desperate Men Do Desperate Things." She reached forward and snapped it off.

"I thought you liked Jimmy LaFave."

"I—I do. I just don't feel like listening to music right now. Do you mind?"

"No, of course not."

Well, aren't we Mr. Accommodating.

Although she kept her face turned away she felt him watching her—studying her. He shifted slightly in his seat. "Jimmy's in town this weekend. At McGonigel's."

"Mmm," she said.

"Have you been there lately?"

"No. I don't go out much."

"I went by and talked to Rusty a couple of days ago. Teresa's pregnant. Twins."

She gasped. *Could he possibly . . . ? No. No way.*

"Are you sure you're all right?"

"Yeah." She turned toward him. "But you've got to admit, Adam. This is pretty awkward. It's ridiculous to act like things are normal between us."

"I know. I'm just glad to see you, to be with you. But you seem, I don't know, really jumpy."

But she looks the same, he thought. Well, almost the same. Thinner. Pale. And he knew she'd been crying. All night long, judging by the way her eyes were puffed up. It had to be that stupid item in the paper. She'd taken off her wedding rings, too. That hurt. Again, he'd bet it was that thing in the paper. Better not to ask about it right now, he thought.

More than anything he wanted to pull the car over, cup her perfect, heart-shaped face in his hands and kiss her silly. He was completely certain if he tried to, she'd slap his face.

He wasn't about to give up, though. They belonged together. Damn it, he loved her, and he knew she still loved him. He'd made a serious miscalculation about how she'd felt about going overseas, but that didn't mean they couldn't go on like before. He was back now. For a little while. He knew he could convince her to join him. After all, they'd been together for years. They were soul mates. He'd never been as close to anyone as he had been to Evie Beauchamp. He knew she felt the same way.

He remembered the day he met her at the Alexanders' house. He'd been at Evansville High School for less than a month, and Louis Alexander had already become a good friend. Still, Adam always hated going to someone's home for the first time—especially the home of someone like Louis Alexander. His father was a doctor and his mother was principal of the elementary school. They were the aristocracy of the small town, and Adam's family was very far removed from those circles.

When they'd walked in through the kitchen, the first thing Adam had seen was the enormous pot of gumbo bubbling on the stove. His spirits had risen considerably. Right next to the stove, a steaming bowl of white fluffy rice sat on an iron trivet. Loaves of crusty French bread were set out along with slabs of real butter, and there were napkins stacked next to a mountain of bowls and plates. The napkins were cloth—blue-and-white checkered. He remembered vividly everything he saw that day.

When the two of them walked through to the family room, Adam saw at least fifteen people sprawled on comfortable-looking furniture, spilling onto the floor and piled together on beat-up beanbag chairs. Everyone was watching *The Wizard of Oz* on Dr. Alexander's new big-screen TV. Adam was introduced around, and though he was able to remember a few of the names—there were five other Alexander children—there were so many neighborhood kids, he couldn't possibly remember who was who. Evie stood out, though.

She was nearly fourteen then, but could have passed for twelve. Or ten. She sat folded up on the divan like a grasshopper, wedged between Mary Margaret and little Hughie Alexander. Her hair was an untamed, ebony corkscrew mane, and she had enormous, jade green eyes. She was stick thin, and Adam's first impression was a black-haired Little Orphan Annie.

Louis stood next to Adam, dutifully intoning names.

"... and Heather, and this is my brother Hughie, and this is Evie Beauchamp—she lives next door—and my sister Mary Margaret—"

"Hey," some fat kid chortled from one of the beanbags. "Adam and Evie. Ha ha ha. Somebody get Evie an apple. Now you'll finally have a boyfriend. Adam and Ee-vie sitting in a tree, K-I-S-S-I—"

The kid might have continued ragging her for a while before the others shushed him, but that didn't happen. Without a second's hesitation, Evie launched herself from the couch and flew through the air, bony arms and legs outstretched like a spider monkey flinging itself from tree to tree. She hit the boy squarely in the gut—a flailing whirlwind of skinny limbs—and had to be pulled away. Adam liked her immediately. He admired a fighter.

Later, after the movie, and replete with several bowls of Mrs. Alexander's spicy seafood gumbo, Adam rose and thanked his hosts. He liked them and he could tell that they liked him, too. They eventually became his surrogate parents, and he lived with them his senior year of high school. But that first night Evie stood up to leave at the same time he did. He knew she'd been watching him during the evening, and had timed her exit to coincide with his. He had smiled inwardly, wondering what had piqued her interest.

He wasn't amused; he was charmed.

"Well," she said, standing and stretching her whippet-thin arms, "I've got to go feed Snoopy."

"You're coming back, aren't you, dear?" Mrs. Alexander asked. Adam heard the protectiveness in the older woman's voice and wondered at it.

"Sure," Evie said. "I gotta go get my stuff."

"Is Snoopy your dog?" Adam asked.

Evie met his gaze, and he realized her eyes looked more emerald close up. "No, Snoopy's my pony. I wish I had a dog, though. That's what I really wanted."

"Boy was she surprised Christmas Day," Hughie said. "She named him Snoopy, anyway, 'cause she'd already picked the name."

"Wow," Adam said. "A pony! Your folks must be really generous to give you a pony when you asked for a dog."

"Not really," she said evenly. "They'd do just about anything to keep me outside."

Adam had started to laugh, but noticed just in time that an awkward silence had fallen in the room. Then he noticed the meaningful glances passing among some of the older people.

"Anyway," she said. "My folks are dead. I live with my Aunt Nila and Uncle Richard. It's the next house, but you can't really see it through the trees."

He noticed that Evie wasn't as young as he'd first thought; she was just small. Her face was serious, and she had fair skin and a wide, intelligent forehead. Her lips were full and curved up naturally—a perfect Cupid's bow mouth, his mother would say. He'd never seen hair so thick and shiny. Thick, sooty lashes fringed her eyes, and her eyebrows arched high and fine on her unfreckled skin.

"Well, I think you're lucky, anyway," he said. "I've never had a pet at all."

She blinked. "Really?"

He nodded. "Really."

"You want to come see Snoopy?" she asked.

"I can't today, but the next time I come I'd like to." She nodded, but he could see that she didn't believe him. He also saw that she accepted it without protest. She was obviously someone who'd grown accustomed to disappointment. At that moment it became vitally important to him not to let her down. He promised he'd go see her pony the very next time he was there. And he'd been true to his word. That time.

Adam sighed. That was ages ago—going on fourteen years. They were so different now. Although Evie looked much the same. She was still girlishly small with enormous green eyes that changed color depending on what she wore. Or her mood. And that hair. She'd tamed her mad curls, and they usually cascaded over her shoulders like a blue-black waterfall, but wet weather gave her fits with it.

He wanted to stare at her, to devour her with his eyes...and hands. After all, he'd been starved for her for months. But the traffic was crawling and the roads were glassy with water. At least she was only a couple of feet away. So close, so close. He wanted to touch her hair and her face, and take her hand in his, but tension rolled off her like high notes on a violin. Something's really wrong, he thought. Maybe she's found somebody else.... His mind slammed shut on the thought. She wouldn't. Not Evie. Not while they were still married.

She took a breath. "So, how long are you supposed to be in town?"

Adam swallowed. This was exactly the question he'd wanted to avoid. "I'm not sure."

She looked at him over her shoulder, and he saw the curve of her lip. She didn't even have to say it out loud. He imagined she was thinking, *Just as I thought.*

"How's the assignment going?" she asked.

Don't lie, just be smart. "Better than I thought. The refinery isn't taking nearly as long as we thought to rework. They'll be at forty percent soon. We hope to be at eighty-five percent in less than six months."

"So everything's working out for you. Just like you hoped."

"No, Evie. Not like I hoped. I want you with me." He took his right hand off the steering wheel. He meant to reach for hers, but she shrank against the door and hugged herself even tighter than before. *God, she won't even let me touch her hand.* Long moments stretched out, measured by the slap of the windshield wipers and the hiss of tires on wet asphalt.

He wanted to get her talking. If only he could capture her interest somehow. God, he'd never felt so awkward—so inept. Surely there was something...
"We go whale watching sometimes. You'd like that."

"Mmm. Whale watching. Sounds fun," she murmured, but Adam could tell she wasn't really paying attention. She'd turned away to trace the falling pattern of rivulets on the window with her finger. When she retreated this way she always struck him as somehow childlike. Not just because she was so little, but long ago he had realized that something inside her had just given up and remained somehow suspended.

He saw it at times like this—the way she would just tune him out and go into herself. Maybe it was losing her parents so young, or being raised by that cold-fish aunt and the demented uncle. Seeing her this way—so out of reach—made him want to gather her to him all the more. To hold her. To lose himself inside her.

"So, tell me," she said presently. "Where are you off to after San Asfallia?"

Adam didn't answer. For years he'd stressed to her that hardship assignments were a shortcut to promotion. But it was more than that. He'd taken difficult assignments because he liked—no, he *needed* the challenge. Ever since he was young, his accomplishments—the evidence of his success—had distanced him from the memory of the grinding poverty he'd grown up in.

At first Evie had understood his need to be challenged, to fight the elements in the oil field and the boardroom. She'd known how the gnawing sense of failure that had always seemed to be waiting to devour him could only have been defeated by achievement. That had been the essence of his personality. He'd known that, and Evie'd known that. She'd taken pride in his drive and ambition. At first. Later on it had forced a wedge between them.

It seemed that as soon as they were married, Evie wanted to settle down—right away—and start having children, even though she knew if they had small children, company policy would exclude Adam from the assignments he wanted. This had been the source of Evie's unhappiness.

God, the arguments they'd had over kids. And after only a couple of years—four or five at the most—she'd just become so stubborn and had refused to see, wouldn't be reasonable or even try to understand at all.

"Well are you going to answer me?" She swung around, and Adam recognized the challenge in her posture. She might as well have said it. *Was it worth the breakup of our marriage? Or does this mean you've decided to come home to stay?* "Where to next? Afghanistan? Ghana?"

God, it was like she was clairvoyant. How many times had they laughed about reading each other's thoughts? But things just weren't that simple.

"I'm not sure, this assignment's not over yet, and I won't know what comes next until we're done. Like I said, we're ahead of schedule—months, but it'll be at least another—"

"I see," she said, and turned away again.

"Evie . . ."

"What? You see? Even now, no matter what you say, work comes first, doesn't it?"

"Why don't you come with me? Just try it, darling. Argentina's not beautiful, but we can travel to other places. I need you with—"

"I want a divorce, Adam," she said. "As soon as possible. Tomorrow. And there's something else you ought to know."

She turned to face him, and when Adam saw her eyes, he almost pulled the car over. The way she looked was almost scary—like a cornered animal—terrified but ready, almost eager to get on with the fight.

"I have a baby, Adam."

Chapter Three

Adam hit the brakes, and the car fishtailed danger-ously. As they slid into the outside lane, a rain-dappled half-ton pickup drifted into Evie's peripheral vision, and she cringed in anticipation. Just in time the driver swerved and avoided them, but his horn blared—al-most in Evie's ear it seemed—and she clutched at the dashboard to brace herself. "What are you doing? Have you lost your mind?"

Adam didn't answer, but his knuckles stood out white against his dark skin as he deftly brought the car back under control and maneuvered across the lanes. Nearly expressionless he coasted into the next park-ing lot they came to without ever saying a word. Evie knew he was dangerously angry.

When the car came to a stop he turned to face her. "What did you say to me?"

"I said, 'Have you lost your mind?'"

"Don't be cute, Evie. What the hell is going on?"

She swallowed and looked around. They were just blocks from the shop, and she knew it would only take a few minutes to walk home. At this point she didn't give a damn if she had to walk in the rain. "I don't want to stop here." She popped her seat belt and reached for the door handle. "If you're not going to—"

She wasn't even aware that he'd moved until his hand clamped down around her wrist. His expression never changed. "You're not going anywhere until you tell me what's going on. What about a baby? Whose baby?"

Evie didn't bother to struggle, instead she faced him square on. "Her name is Juliette, and I'm adopting her. Her mother is—was—my roommate. Don't worry, Adam, she's not your responsibility. Nothing is going to stand in the way of your career."

"Wait a minute. Did you say her mother *was* . . ."?

"Yes." Evie made a point of looking down at her wrist, not only because she wanted him to let go, she also knew she couldn't look him in the face—not now, not with what she had to say next. "Her name was Marlene Hitchcock," she said softly. "Marlene's dead."

Adam loosened his fingers, and Evie snatched her arm back into her lap. "But . . . the father? Isn't there some family or—?"

"No. No family. No father." She faced him again. "*He* didn't want children, either."

Anger flashed across Adam's face. "Don't start with me, Evie. You know I want to have children someday."

She let the corner of her mouth curl. "Right."

This was very old territory.

"So," he said slowly, "you're adopting this baby—"

"Yes. Can we start moving, now? I was supposed to be home more than an hour ago to feed her."

"Who's taking care of . . . Julianne?"

"Juliette. Olivia Delcomb is watching her for me right now. Olivia owns the shop where I work. She's also my friend."

Adam started the car and pulled back into the stream of traffic. He looked white. Evie could see him thinking, trying to process the information and make it somehow work for him and fit into his plans. It wouldn't, though. Not ever.

"And you take the baby to work with you?"

"Well, sort of. There's a duplex over the shop. We, the baby and I, live in one half. Olivia lives in the other. She's wonderful. *She's* been there for both of us all along." Evie knew he'd recognize the accusation, but of course he couldn't acknowledge it. "You turn right up there by the—"

"I know," he snapped.

Adam had never liked her giving directions. Evie, however, didn't indulge herself in a moment of smugness. She was almost sick with relief that he finally knew about the baby. Now all she had to do was get home and get away from him.

Adam said nothing for the last few moments of the drive, and Evie sat quietly, hoping that he'd just accept what she'd told him and go away. She had a sinking feeling that it wasn't going to be quite that easy to get rid of him. As soon as he pulled into the shallow parking lot in front of the shop, she jumped out. "Thanks for the ride. I'll call you tomorrow to talk about... arrangements."

He just stared at her and reached down for his cellular phone. "I have to make a call, Evie, but I'll be right in."

"You can't...I mean, I have to get to work. This is my job, and I have to... you can't just..."

He didn't even answer her, but just held the phone loosely in one hand. She knew it was hopeless. She turned and fled up the steps, hoping against hope that the baby was asleep and that Olivia wasn't busy.

Steep gables and ornate gingerbread wood trim made Something Different one of the most authentic looking of the restored Victorian houses in Montrose. Its hipped roof sheltered a deep wraparound porch, cluttered with Olivia's potted trees, white wicker furniture and Boston ferns. Eighty-year-old oaks shaded the little parking lot, and their gnarled roots had pushed up through the sidewalk in a show of inexorable power, but their arms arched almost delicately over the street to brush the leaf tips of their sisters on the other side of Westheimer.

Evie threaded her way quickly through the chairs, and her wet sneakers thumped hollowly on the porch. Copper cowbells rattled when she pulled the door open and burst into the shop. As always she was struck first by the scents she loved and had help choose: eucalyptus, vanilla, patchouli.

When she'd first come to work at Something Different, Olivia's store was well established, but it lacked a certain spark. Evie brought not only her artist's eye and education, but countless small treasures she'd accumulated over the years, as well as antiques uncovered during endless market stall excursions. She'd insisted that Olivia take a percentage from each sale of her own things, but over the past months the shop had begun to be more of a partnership between the two women.

"Olivia!"

She appeared at the door that separated the large main room from the kitchen, which now functioned as the office. As soon as she saw Evie, relief flooded her features. "Evie, thank God. I was so worried. I called—"

"Adam's here. Just outside. He's coming in. He brought me home."

"Oh, my God. But where's the—?"

"I ran into him at the office. Can you believe it? It was like a nightmare. We got stuck in the elevator together."

"I know. They told me."

"Who told you?"

"When you were gone so long I called to see if you'd made it to the office, and the girl I spoke with— some horribly rude little cow—anyway, she told me you'd just left with Adam."

"Where's Juliette?"

"Sleeping. I fed her and—"

"Oh, thanks, Olivia. Listen, do you think you—?"

At that moment the bells at the door rattled and Adam walked in. Evie knew she and Olivia were both standing stiff as statues from panic and probably owl-eyed as well. Adam, on the other hand, closed the door and strode forward confidently, smoothly—as if he belonged there or had been expected. Evie felt a surge of irritation. But somehow, at the same time, she felt the oddest little twinge of pride.

She had always been proud to introduce Adam to her friends. He was an extremely handsome and masculine man, in the prime of his life. His rough-cut sable hair was thick as a pelt, and he oozed self-confidence softened by an almost boyish charm. Though his smile wasn't perfect, his teeth were white, and the creases at the corners of his eyes gave his good looks character.

He held out his hand. "Mrs. Delcomb? I'm Adam Rabalais."

His words broke the spell of immobility that had held them, and Evie was aware that they'd both been holding their breaths. She started speaking in a rush, but realized Olivia was doing the same thing.

"I'm sorry, Adam . . . Olivia. I should have—"

"It's nice to meet you. Evie has told me—"

Evie looked at Olivia. Olivia looked back at her. She hoped she didn't look as pale and flustered as her friend, but she had a sinking suspicion that she did. An awkward silence stretched out.

Olivia cleared her throat.

"I'm sorry," Evie began slowly. "I should have spoken up." She turned slightly. "Adam, this is my friend and the owner of Something Different, Olivia Delcomb. Olivia, this is my... Adam Rabalais."

"I'm pleased to meet you, Mr. Rabalais," Olivia said, her native grace apparently intact.

"Thank you, but please call me Adam," he replied. "I feel as if I already know you. Evie's told me a lot about you in a short amount of time. You know, I noticed this shop a while back and I always meant to stop in. It looks really intriguing from the street. Such a great looking old house. Do you stay very busy?"

"Well," said Olivia, warming to her topic, "I can't complain. Things have been picking up steadily. Evie has so many wonderful ideas, and she's so creative."

Thank you, Olivia. Now please help me get rid of him.

"Have you been here very long?" Adam asked.

Olivia, however, blossomed garrulously under Adam's interest. With a shy but graceful turn of her hand, she summed up her little business—the antiques, herbs and dried flowers, the books and eclectic jumble of objets d'art collected to embellish their creations. "My grandfather built this house in nineteen hundred, right after the Great Storm in Galveston, and I was born in the gabled, corner bedroom. I'm seventh-generation Texas, you know, and the only time in my life I ever moved away from this house..."

Evie watched with dismay as Adam trained on Olivia his massive charm and undivided interest. She'd seen this happen dozens of times. He had the uncanny ability to make anyone he spoke with feel that each and every word said to him was important, engrossing and of momentous consequence to his life.

The odd thing was he usually felt that way. Adam liked people, and they liked him back. There was a time that this quality had delighted her.

At that moment, however, Evie wanted him to go away. She itched to go into the kitchen and peek at the baby, but she was afraid Adam might follow her. Lifting her arm, she made an elaborate show of checking her watch. Surely Olivia would take the hint. Unfortunately the older woman never even hesitated.

Adam had his head tipped slightly to the side, as he apparently hung on every word she said.

For Pete's sake, Olivia, can't you see what he's doing?

Evie's stomach was beginning to burn, and not only because she'd missed breakfast and lunch. The morning had exhausted her, and though the accidental meeting with Adam hadn't been a complete disaster, she'd had enough for one day. She wanted a glass of wine, a microwave pizza and a chance to tell Olivia everything that had happened. "Well," she said, turning toward Adam, "I hate to rush off, but I've got work to do."

Adam cocked his head her way, but didn't take his attention away from Olivia who was midway into a family history lesson. Olivia blushed slightly and stammered into silence. "Oh, I—I am running on, aren't I?"

"Not at all," Adam said. "I love family stories."

"Shall I walk you to your car?" Evie asked firmly.

Adam's mouth tightened almost imperceptibly, and the slightest tick at the corner of his eye told Evie he wasn't nearly as composed as he'd seemed. Years of poker-faced negotiating, as well as his natural sang-froid, hardly ever failed him, but Evie saw that he was at a loss. She felt the beginnings of exhilaration. She had control of the situation. It was just possible that she was going to pull it off.

"Umm," Olivia said tentatively, "I—I'm sorry but...what happened to the van?"

Evie's hands flew to her face. "Oh, my God. The van. Olivia, I'm so sorry. They towed it. I'll go call. I've got the—"

"It's on its way back," Adam said.

Both women turned to face him.

"I called from my car phone. My secretary's getting in touch with the towing company, and they're bringing it back here. It shouldn't be too long."

"But...how—?" Evie was stammering, her moment of exhilaration had dissolved once again into a feeling of helplessness.

"Why was it towed?" Olivia asked.

"I double parked when I was—"

"They're really strict about it," Adam interjected. "It happens all the time. Anyway, don't worry about it. The company is picking up the charge."

"Well, thank you," Olivia said. "I—that's awfully kind of you, but are you sure—?"

"My pleasure," Adam said. "I'm glad I had a chance to meet you."

Olivia was wringing her hands with relief. "Well, I really appreciate your doing that for me. May I offer you a cup of coffee or something before you go?"

Olivia! Evie glared at her friend. Olivia shrugged a little as if to say, *I have to be gracious. After all...*

Evie's stomach did a sickening roll. What if the baby woke up? What if Adam—?

"Why don't you show Adam the sitting room?" Olivia said. "I'll bring a tray right in."

"Right." Evie turned and walked toward the old foyer. A cherry wood banister curved up to the second floor, and framed portraits and photographs stared down benignly from Olivia's flocked wallpaper. Ferns cascaded from their antique stands, and an enormous, hanging Tiffany lamp showered them with fractured light.

"This is pretty," Adam said.

"Mmm."

Antiques cluttered the parlor, and before Adam could plant himself on one of the love seats, Evie steered him toward a round, claw-footed dining table, which she knew had extremely uncomfortable chairs. When he sat down, she took the chair farthest from him. He looked at her sadly.

"Why are you doing this?"

Evie's throat closed, and she looked at her hands. "Don't you think this is hard for me, too?"

"Well, then why don't you—"

"Please don't," she said, and pressed the heels of her hands against her eyes. "I'm worn out. I've had a horrible day. Please don't make me..." Her voice was going, thinning out to a pathetic girlish parody. She took a deep, shuddering breath and suddenly he was there, not daring to touch her, but still somehow offering the comfort of his warm presence. She hadn't even heard him move to the chair next to her.

"Evie," he murmured. She felt a soothing touch between her shoulders, just below the knot of her hair.

In a moment of weakness she allowed herself to be drawn toward him. She hadn't realized how clenched she'd been until every rigid muscle in her shoulders collapsed into his arms—into the embrace where she had always felt small and protected. His smell was so familiar—the old-fashioned soap he used, the distant wintery cologne, the fine, soft wool of his suit. He sighed into her hair and moved one broad, comforting hand to the nape of her neck.

Some faraway part of Evie's mind sounded a warning, but she ignored it, and long-dormant nerve endings roused, flexed and nudged at sleeping impulses. Evie surrendered to impulse, opened her arms and rested her palms against his shirt. So wonderfully familiar—the curve of his ribs, the distant rush of breath and the quiet thunder of his heart.

"Here we go." Olivia breezed in, balancing a tray. "Such a gloomy day, isn't it? There's nothing quite like—"

Evie pulled away from Adam and sat up.

The smile fell from Olivia's face. "Oh, I—I'm sorry."

"No," Evie said, and stood so fast the clawed feet of her chair shrieked on the hardwood floor. "I need to get to work." She didn't look at Adam. "I'll leave the two of you to visit." She backed away and stood on the opposite side of the table. "Adam can tell you about his wedding plans."

That comment had the same effect as a hand grenade rolling into the room. The tray slipped from Olivia's hands and hit the table with a crash. Adam jumped up shouting. "Damn it, Evie. You know perfectly well that I'm not engaged to anyone."

The bells in the next room clanged, and Olivia flinched, then fled muttering, "I'm sorry, please excuse me."

For a long moment they stared at each other across the table, and Evie felt the tension between them intensifying like a static charge. She faced him as long as she could, but this kind of confrontation was Adam's style and she couldn't keep it up. She let her shoulders sag. She was just too tired.

"It doesn't matter, anyway," she said. "I want you to talk to Tony in your office about filing for divorce. I'll sign whatever I'm supposed to sign and you can...do whatever has to be done after that. I'm moving back to Evansville."

"*Evansville?*" Adam's face was a portrait of incredulity. "What the hell are you going to do in Evansville? There's nothing there."

Evie swallowed. "I'm going to raise Juliette, and I'm going to open a shop like this one."

Adam's eyes narrowed. "Wait a minute," he said skeptically, "you're going to adopt a baby, but you're going to leave the state? How can you—?"

"Don't worry about that," Evie said, cutting her eyes away. "I'll take care of all that. I just want you to get the divorce started. I'll take care of everything else. I don't have much of anything left in the house—"

"Couldn't we try counseling or something?"

"Hah! Don't you remember? I tried to get you to go three years ago. You immediately went to Kenya for six weeks."

"I don't want a divorce, Evie." He gave her a determined look. "I'm going to fight it."

She hardened her gaze. "Then we have nothing to talk about. If you won't help me, we'll just have to hire lawyers and let them do all the communicating."

"All right," he snapped. "I'll do what you want, but this doesn't mean for one minute that I—"

"Excuse me, Adam." Olivia stood at the door, wringing her hands and scarlet with embarrassment. "I'm sorry, but the tow truck is here with the van, and they want to pull into the parking lot, but your car is blocking the driveway."

"It's okay," he said. "I'm just leaving." He was suddenly composed, and Evie felt an odd sinking. He was taking this much too easily. It simply wasn't like him.

He paused in the arched doorway and took Olivia's hand. "It was nice meeting you. I hope I'll see you again."

"Oh, I'm just sure of it. I just know we're going to be—I mean I really enjoyed . . ." she stammered into silence.

He turned back. "I'll be in touch, Evie."

She nodded but didn't meet his eyes. Instead she looked down at the table where the coffee and spilled milk were spreading in a muddy pool on the little tray. The bells told her when he opened the door, and then his hard, quick steps pounded on the wooden porch. In moments an engine snarled to life.

Evie walked to the window and watched him back into the street and then ease forward into the traffic. Olivia stood at her shoulder.

Evie swallowed the ache in her throat. "He didn't—he didn't even ask to see her."

Olivia reached out and touched her arm. "That's not unusual. Men never show much interest in other people's—I mean, I suppose you told him—"

"I told him Marlene died, and I was adopting the baby."

Olivia sighed and looked back to where Adam's car had disappeared down the street. "He looked furious."

Evie almost laughed. "He wasn't mad. He was just frustrated because he wasn't getting his way and he couldn't do anything about it."

Olivia's brows rose. "He looked awfully mad to me."

"Sometime," Evie said softly, "sometime I'll tell you what he's like when he loses his temper." She turned toward her friend. "Do we have any wine?"

Olivia nodded.

"Do you mind if I drink on the job?"

Olivia smiled. "I'll join you. My nerves are shot."

Evie gathered up the coffee things, and while Olivia opened a bottle of Chablis and poured two glasses, Evie checked on the baby.

Juliette slept sprawled in the shameless oblivion of the very young. As always the sight of the baby's perfect and undisturbed innocence left Evie both humbled and more than a little afraid.

Am I going to be a good mother? What if something happens to me? Who'll take care of her?

Sometimes her fears overwhelmed her, but there were other moments—moments of private magic—when she was overcome with awe and gratitude. She would sit for an hour just rocking the baby and lose herself in studying the tiny, perfect fingernails, the pink shell of her ear or the lashes feathered against her peach-soft skin.

Completely unaware, Juliette slept soundly on her back in Olivia's hundred-year-old Shaker cradle. One tiny fist lay against her cheek, and her cap of dark curls made a blue-black halo against the pale, flannel sheets.

Olivia appeared quietly at Evie's shoulder and handed her a cool goblet. "Here."

"Thanks," Evie whispered. "She's so little. What if I can't—I mean, I'm always wondering if I can..." She sighed. "It all scares me. I'm afraid I'll do a bad job."

"I know exactly how you feel. Raising a baby is scary. But you'll be a wonderful mother. You already are." Olivia tapped her glass with her fingernails. "Evie, you know I would never question your personal decisions, but as your friend...I mean, because you're somebody I really care about I have to—"

"I know what you're going to say." Evie didn't face her friend. "He does seem to be a wonderful man, doesn't he? But you've only seen him when he's trying to be charming. Trying to get what he wants."

"He really did seem so—I don't know—intent on you."

At that moment Juliette stirred. She arched her tiny back and her face reddened in a grimace as she struck at the air with one arm and turned her head angrily.

Evie reached into the cradle with her free hand and made soothing, cooing noises as she gently stroked the baby's tummy. "Hush now. Shh."

Silky, blue-black lashes fluttered against perfect alabaster skin, and the baby's eyes opened—sleepy, outraged eyes that searched and blinked and fought the burden of exhaustion.

Rain-colored eyes.

Rabalais eyes.

Chapter Four

Adam rubbed his eyes. "There's got to be something I can do about this," he muttered. His frustration had balled itself into a hard knot right in the middle of his chest. He checked his watch. Not quite four o'clock. There was still time to make some calls and talk to Martin about the pipeline leases. That is, if he could get his damn concentration back. He glanced at the sky in irritation.

The rain had diminished to a listless drizzle, but gray clouds were still clamped down over the city like an ugly helmet, and the weather reports promised at least another week of it. Adam hated the gloom of a wet fall. He used to like rainy weather, but he couldn't really remember why, and there damn sure didn't seem to be much good about it now.

He rolled his shoulders. He'd had a lousy night's sleep. Again. He just couldn't get used to sleeping without Evie. The slapped-up, prefab housing at San Asfallia had been bad enough, but sleeping without her in the house they'd shared here was worse. He could hardly stand to be at home at all.

If he sat in the den, all he could see was Evie's pretty garden overgrown and gone all straggly. The whole house seemed to be coated with the film of dust that settles in rooms not used very much. The bedroom was the worst of all, silent and haunted with memories. He'd been home for weeks, and it wasn't getting better.

He'd told himself time and again that it was only temporary. Maybe, he thought, just maybe I'm handling this the wrong way. Nah, he told himself. If there was one lesson he'd learned by the time he was thirteen years old, it was to be patient and never take no for an answer. If you stay your course and wait it out, you'll get what you were after.

That strategy had always worked before.

Of course, he'd been struggling with the same problem for months. The whole time he'd been gone he'd expected her to quit being so damn stubborn and join him. Evie was the most obstinate person he'd ever met in his life. But even Evie had never stayed mad this long before. Still, he hadn't really become worried until she'd stopped taking his calls. Then she'd moved out of the house and pulled the silly stunt of trying to hide from him. Now that had scared him.

Even after all that, he was ready to forgive and forget. Hell, he didn't even expect an apology. He just wanted his wife back. No matter how demanding and unreasonable she'd become over the past couple of years.

Lately he'd even had the nagging suspicion that maybe some of this trouble between them really was his fault. He wondered if maybe, just maybe, he *had* been neglecting her too much and spending too much energy on his career. He swiped the thought away immediately. He hadn't changed. She had. God, thinking about it made his head ache.

He was worn out. Every movement seemed forced, and his eyes felt grainy all the time. This was more than jet lag and long hours. This was a bone-deep weariness that didn't go away no matter how much he tried to rest. Of course, he hadn't slept more than three hours at a time since he'd landed in Houston.

The dreams had started recurring irregularly months ago, right after he'd started in San Asfallia, but now it seemed every night, the minute he closed his eyes, his childhood nightmares came crushing down in an avalanche of hideous images. Maybe it was being home again that had brought them back or being alone in the house he'd always shared with Evie. The cause of the nightmares didn't really matter, the fact was that he was getting close to the end of his rope.

He'd first had the dreams almost twenty-five years ago when his family lived in Marline, Texas. Curtis Rabalais had moved his wife and children there when he got a job doing work-overs on land rigs. The only place they could find to rent was a two-bedroom single-wide trailer, so all the kids had to share a room.

Clyde Allison's eighty-acre cow pasture separated the mobile homes from the decent peoples' houses in the Ridgewood Manor Edition, and the railroad tracks kept the trailer park from spurting over the highway and spreading farther west. A gravel quarry was scooped out on the far side of the highway as a further discouragement in case the low-income housing suddenly tried to spread like some kind of fungus.

The Rabalais trailer was one of about fifty that were available for short-term lease in Lloyd's Trailer Park, and was flanked by the Mar-Tex Refinery on one side and railroad tracks on the other. Lloyd's was no worse than many of the places where Adam's family had lived and was even better than some, although Adam had never lived so close to a railroad track before.

He had a panoramic view of the refinery and the railroad tracks because, being the oldest, he got the top bunk by the window. Every night as he lay there he heard the inevitable groan and distant, ugly whistle that meant another train was coming. It always seemed to be in the dark thin hours after midnight that a diesel engine would roar by with a prehistoric scream, shaking the trailer and rattling the cheap, shiny paneling in the room Adam shared with his brother and the girls.

The noise never seemed to bother the younger kids. They slept sprawled and oblivious no matter how horrible the racket got. But the trains never failed to wake Adam. He just knew that someday an engine full of acid or something worse was going to jump its tracks, plow through the rickety trailer park and throw them all sky high like the wooden pins at the Lucky Bowl.

The refinery also added its own malign signature to Adam's nights. After dark—less than a quarter of a mile away—the bare bulbs lining the towers and catalytic cracking units blinked like greasy stars, and a fog of yellow safety light puddled like mustard gas on the asphalt decks below.

Adam would lie awake listening to the steel wheels shrieking, and as if in answer—late and far beyond the observation of the environmental authorities—Mar-Tex would flare off spent gas. Trails of fire streamed across the black sky and filled the little room with the roar of uncocked gas jets and hideous, undulating orange light.

"This is what hell is like," he told himself, as night after night, he lay awake, caught between the screaming trains and the apocalyptic glow of the flares. "Maybe I'm already dead and this is hell." He scared himself so badly, sometimes he would lie in bed and shake. When it got really bad the shaking woke up Earl, who would whine and have to be brought water, so Adam trained himself to lie still.

Eventually he could lie motionless, eyes wide and staring, for as long as it took the trains to go by. Later on he could do it anytime he was scared—go still and wide-eyed, not really seeing or hearing—just waiting for the horror to pass.

Eventually he began to think someone was trying to tell him something. Lying there listening to the rattle of the wheels, he sensed an urgent and personal message. That was the worst, to lie there possum still, listening and straining to understand what the forces in the universe were trying to tell him. Night after night it was always the same.

And then one sweltering June day, when he and Earl were walking down the track berry picking, they ran into Beth Ann Culotta. Beth Ann's father was Lloyd Culotta who owned the trailer park. And Lloyd's Real Estate. And about a third of everything else worth owning in Jacksonboro County. Although Adam had only gone to Marline Middle School for the last six weeks of the semester, he'd noticed Beth Ann right away.

Beth Ann had colored hair bands to match all her tennis shoes, and she wore those up-to-date plastic watches in every color you could imagine. She had small, slim hands, and her bright, chestnut hair swung like a shining tassel when she walked down the hallway with her giggling friends. She was the most beautiful thing Adam and ever seen. And she may as well have been from another planet.

The Culotta family lived in the old part of Marline in a house with a paddock for Beth Ann's pony, and a four-car garage for Mr. Culotta's stock race cars. That Sunday Beth Ann was visiting her father's less-well-off sister, Vonda Birchwood, in Ridgewood Manor.

"Hi," she said, sliding her brown eyes up at him.

Adam nodded. "Hi."

"Y'all gettin' many?"

He didn't reply aloud, but instead hefted the five-pound coffee can and showed her that it was more than halfway full of dark, fat berries with tight skins ready to burst with purple juice.

"My Aunt Vonda says there's snakes around here."

"I like snakes," Adam lied.

"Me, too," Earl said. "I like 'em lots."

Beth Ann wrinkled her freckled nose. "Not me. They scare me to pieces."

"You want some?" Adam asked. "We already got nearly enough for a cobbler, and we haven't even been picking an hour."

"Well," she said, "can't I just come with y'all and help?"

And at that moment it seemed to Adam that the clouds parted, and he heard the swell of the heavenly choir, and he nearly fell to his knees in gratitude for the unexpected kindness of the benevolent universe. Within an hour he had been invited to go swimming with Beth Ann and her family that very afternoon at the Bayou Cay Country Club in a real swimming pool—not the beach, a swimming hole or canal, but a real swimming pool with a diving board and a concession stand. Adam gave Beth Ann the whole can of berries and lit out for home. Earl, red-faced and indignant at not being included, had to keep up as best he could.

Adam burst through the metal door of the trailer and let it wham shut behind him. He knew that got on his mother's nerves, but he had transcended himself with euphoria. "I'm going swimming, Mama," he huffed. "I got to get me a swimming suit. Fast."

Naomi Rabalais looked up from her ironing, pursed her lips and shoved at her hair with the back of her wrist. "What's wrong with your cutoffs?"

He explained where he was going, and his mother, who understood these things, walked him to Lloyd's Quickie Pickie and spent more than she should have on blue swimming trunks decorated with big yellow fish. Adam didn't care for the fish motif, but it was either the yellow fish or his cutoffs, and he knew as well as any ignoramus that you can't wear cutoffs in a real swimming pool.

Adam also didn't have the right shoes or a good towel but he had to make do. Naomi seemed as happy as he was that he'd been invited somewhere nice, and she gave him a dollar fifty in change to buy something for Beth Ann at the concession stand. Of course, there wasn't enough for both of them, and he knew it meant he would have to go without, but he understood that the man sometimes had to do that. It showed politeness not to be greedy.

He wrapped his money up in his towel and ran back down the tracks to Beth Ann's aunt's house. The pink brick two-story had square columns and a deep slab porch decorated with white, uncomfortable-looking furniture that Adam suspected no one ever sat on. Cast iron deer with short legs and huge ears stood in the middle of the lawn, looking startled and completely ridiculous. Adam waited until he'd caught his breath to ring the bell, and when the door swung open, a woman in an Easter-egg yellow dress stood there looking down at him.

"Yes?"

"Umm, I'm Adam Rabalais, ma'am," he said, holding his towel tight against his stomach. "I'm supposed to go swimming with Beth Ann at the country club." He spread his arms a little so she could see that he was properly dressed.

There was a moment of silence, and Adam saw the slight ascension of penciled brows followed by the almost imperceptible narrowing of the blue-shadowed eyes. "Oh, is that so?" she said. "And where did you come from?"

"The trailer park, ma'am" he replied, tilting his head over his shoulder. He felt the slightest tremor in his joy. "Just up there. You know."

As she nodded, Beth Ann appeared behind her. "Hi, Adam," she said, and her eyes darted up toward the woman and back again. "You all ready?" she asked. Everyone stood very still, but Beth Ann's voice wobbled as if she'd caught the same thing that was causing Adam's middle to feel light and queasy.

"Elizabeth Ann Culotta," the woman said, as she rounded on the girl, "good-night nurse, what on God's green earth are you thinking of? If you think I'm going to show up at Bayou Cay Country Club dragging some poor, white trailer trash along, you must be out of your cotton-pickin' mind. Your daddy would have a conniption fit, and I'd never hear the end of it from your mama. She'd never invite me again."

Her tirade went on for some minutes after that, but Adam didn't hear the whole conversation, even though Beth Ann's Aunt Vonda didn't bother to close the door or even try to keep him from hearing every word. Adam felt the words thump into him like arrows. Trailer trash. He heard the echo as he walked back to Lloyd's Trailer Park.

Trailer trash. It gouged a place in his middle and echoed in his head and scuttled around inside his body leaving black marks every place it hit. His mother didn't even ask what had happened when he came back in. She just watched and let him walk back to his room.

That was the first night he dreamed that the train jumped its tracks. And this time it wasn't a diesel engine but an old-fashioned steam locomotive with a deep cow catcher in front like huge teeth and trails of fire and black smoke boiling out of the stack. A woman in an Easter-egg yellow dress balanced on the rim of the cow catcher, dancing with malice and pointing the way for the blind monster, and Adam heard over and over again the voice of the grinding wheels speaking plainly at last.

Trailer trash, trailer trash.

And at last he heard and understood.

Adam rubbed his eyes again, trying to ease the spiking pain. All that was so long ago. He was a completely different person now. Although the dreams had haunted him for years, he'd found ways to make the voices in his head quiet down. Over the years he'd finally been able to shut them up altogether.

In the meantime he'd achieved every goal he'd ever set for himself. A full scholarship to LSU. Graduation with honors. Athletic awards. Professional achievements. Friends. And a gorgeous wife—his childhood friend and sweetheart, who knew and understood the landscape of his soul.

Why would she leave him now, he wondered, when everything they'd worked for was within reach? What had made Evie change toward him and turn her back on everything they'd built together? He sighed. He was too tired to think about it, but one thing was for sure, he wasn't going back to South America without her. Part of himself was missing without her. God, if he went back without her, he'd probably never get a full night's sleep again.

And what about this baby she was adopting? Thinking about it gave him a sinking feeling in his gut, like the moment when an airliner falls in an air pocket. He couldn't understand her actions. He knew Evie wanted kids. There'd been times when it was all she'd talk about, but to take someone else's child to raise? And what about that woman—Marlene Hitchcock? The whole situation seemed weird. And vaguely illegal. Well, he'd talk to Tony about drawing up some papers so Evie would think he was complying with her wishes. But he was damn sure going to have Tony do some research about just taking over someone else's orphaned child.

He sighed. He'd never thought Evie would have been able to turn him away once she'd seen him face-to-face. The ache in his middle spread through his torso and made his gut burn. He'd been so close to her. He'd touched her, just for a moment, but something of her still lingered faintly on his clothes, in his car. He took a deep breath and raked his hair.

She still loves me, I can feel it, he thought. If she didn't, I'd know. He clamped his jaw. Well, damn it, this isn't going to happen. I won't let it. He tightened his hands around the steering wheel. He would simply not have it any other way. After all, she wanted him; he knew it. And *he* had never wanted anything so much in his life.

"Adam doesn't want children, Olivia. He never did." Evie turned to her friend and kept her voice low but urgent. "I grew up around someone who didn't want me—my uncle. I told you, he despised me and hated having me around. From the time I was five years old, I was treated like an inconvenience—an intrusion. You wouldn't believe the things he said to me and the way he made me feel. I was just a baby myself. You can't imagine what it's like to be raised in a house where you're unwanted."

Olivia sighed. "Did Adam always say he never wanted to have a family?"

"Oh, no. He said he wanted children *someday*. It's just that someday never came. And believe me, no one is going to treat my baby the way I was treated. Not even if it's her father."

"But, Evie, are you sure? How can you not tell him—?"

"Because I know exactly what he'd do. If he found out Juliette was his daughter, he'd take charge right away. He'd withdraw from the overseas assignments, step out of the fast track with his career, and he'd be totally financially and physically accountable for her." Evie stopped and looked Olivia dead in the eye. "And he would make her life hell. And mine. She'd know, just like I knew, that she was in the way, that she ruined everything, that she stood in the path of his one true love—his career.''

"Oh, honey, are you sure?''

"Yeah," she said softly. "I'm sorry to say I've never been more sure of anything in my life. I can't let it happen to her, too, Livvie." Evie swallowed incipient tears. "One time, when I was about nine I went in to Richard's study and asked him to let me be adopted. You know what? He laughed. He said, 'What makes you think anyone would want *you?*'" She took a shuddering breath. "Children know when they're not wanted. At least this way Juliette will grow up with at least one parent who wants her and loves her more than anything in the world.''

Olivia sighed. "I'm sorry. I just can't believe that anyone could look at this precious angel and not adore her.''

"Well," Evie said bitterly, "you grew up another way. You raised your family in another world.''

"So you're not even going to give Adam a chance?''

"It's not a matter of *giving* a chance. It's *taking* a chance. And I just can't.''

The baby sighed and slipped back into a fitful sleep, and Evie motioned for Olivia to follow her out. They sat down at the long kitchen table, and Evie traced a pattern in the moisture on her glass. "In a way I'm glad this happened today. I was going to have to face him sooner or later, and I probably would have put it off for too long.''

She shrugged. "Now I'll have to go forward with the plan. I know this is hard for you to understand, Livvie, but don't you see? I can't take a chance on what Adam will do. Juliette is innocent of everything that happened to both of us, but she'd suffer for it. I can't roll the dice and just hope that he suddenly changes his mind and decides to become a devoted father. And certainly not if the dice I'm rolling are Juliette's heart and soul.''

Olivia shook her head. "And you're absolutely sure that he'll resent her?"

Evie nodded and tried to keep the bitterness out of her voice. "You know I never like talking about this, but when I found out I was pregnant, I called him in Mexico. It was in February—no, January—after last Christmas. After the robbery. I wanted to tell him, but he'd just gotten the news about being assigned to that stupid San Asfallia Refinery project. A three-year assignment. He'd been angling for a job like that for a couple of years, but the company doesn't give those assignments to men with small children because the living conditions are too rough. They've had so many guys give up because of family strain, they don't even consider family men anymore. Anyway, when he told me, I said, 'But that's three years. Suppose I accidentally get pregnant? What happens then?'"

Evie's voice began to wobble. "You know what he said to me? His voice got really hard and mean, and he said, 'Don't you ruin this for me, Evie. I won't forgive you if you do.'"

"Oh, honey, surely he didn't mean that. It was just mad talk."

"Oh, yes, he did." Evie looked out the window, at the gray light of the fading afternoon. "My uncle used to say that to me all the time. 'You ruined everything.

I'll never forgive you for it.'" Evie looked at her friend. "No one's ever going to say that to my baby. Ever."

"So what's next?"

Evie got up, crossed to the sink and rinsed out her glass. "Adam's got a friend in the law department at Van Kyle. He'll draw up the divorce papers. In the meantime, I guess I'd better get ready to move back to Louisiana. Fast."

Olivia turned her wineglass between her fingers. "I don't want you to go. You're like one of my own daughters."

"I don't want to go, either, but Adam won't leave me alone now that he's found out where we are. I know him. And once he sees Juliette—once he sees those eyes—he'll know without a shadow of doubt whose baby she is."

"That's true," Olivia murmured. She looked up. "Will you be able to make it financially?"

Evie shrugged. "I'll do okay. I can sell the rest of my jewelry."

Olivia shook her head. "Well, all right, but who's going to help you with the baby? You can't do everything yourself."

"I'll live close to the Alexanders. God knows they've been my surrogate parents since I was six." She crossed her arms and leaned against the sink. "And I think I'll do pretty well. Evansville is getting some spillover from New Orleans, and I'll be the only one with a business like this. I have you to thank for this idea. I never thought I could do anything with a fine arts degree except make entertaining chitchat at cock-

tail parties. Since I'll be able to keep Juliette with me,
I won't have to pay for child care. I'll do okay.''

"You still have your aunt and uncle there, too.
You're closer to them now.''

"Well, for whatever that's worth. But I'll never be
really close to them, and I can hardly imagine my Aunt
Nila popping over with a big plate of cookies and an
offer to baby-sit. She's always been totally wrapped up
in Uncle Richard's life. And he—well, I've told you
about him. When I told my aunt the Marlene Hitchcock story, she didn't question what I was doing, but
I had the definite feeling she was biting her tongue.''

Olivia stood. "This is the last time I'm going to
mention it, but you know once you start telling lies—
once you take liberties with the truth—these things
snowball. You're going to have to lie on those divorce
papers, you know.''

Evie shrugged. "I'm willing to do whatever I have
to do to protect my child. No one is ever going to hurt
her. Not as long as there's something I can do about
it.''

For the next three days Evie felt as if she were
walking on eggshells. Every time the phone rang she
was afraid to pick it up, but Adam never called her.
Sometimes she had the oddest feeling that he was
thinking about her, trying to probe her mind from a
distance and find out what she was thinking and doing.

She made a halfhearted attempt at organizing her
things to get ready to move, but she was always so
tired. Every night, after feeding and bathing the baby

and doing a load or two of clothes, all she wanted to do was fall into bed and drift into a nice, peaceful coma.

On Friday a cold front blew down from the north and turned the October air crisp and blue. Despite the glorious weather, Evie's nerves were beginning to fray, and she almost thought of calling Adam to see if he'd made any progress with his lawyer friend. Though she felt tense, she knew at least she looked better. Her hair finally surrendered to a good, hot, blow drying, and the puffy circles under her eyes had faded.

"Do you have any plans for this weekend?" Olivia asked, as she sorted through a box of tin ornaments.

"Well, I've got to get my car inspected and I've got a coupon for Family Jewels, so I thought I'd get Juliette's picture done."

A gleeful gurgle erupted from the clicking swing, next to the table, and Evie turned to her daughter. "Yes, precious, we're talking about you. Do you want to go to the mall with your mama?" She cooed and fussed at the baby, whose head made awkward, clumsy attempts to follow the sound of her mother's voice.

The bells on the front door rattled, and Olivia stood. "My turn," she said. "I'll get it."

Evie bent down and teased the baby's wispy forelock into a sassy comma on her forehead. Juliette had been born with a full head of black curls and, despite the pediatrician's dire prediction, she hadn't lost a hair. "Guess what, sweetie?" Evie cooed, "Mama is going to dress you in that sweet yellow bunny dress from Aunt Livvie, and I'm gonna tape a little bow on your precious head for your picture." Funny, she thought, how Adam hated the color yellow, and Evie had always thought it so cheery.

Olivia's voice drifted in from the foyer, high-pitched and a little shrill. Evie stopped and listened for a moment, and when she heard the rumble of a masculine voice in reply, she stiffened. The sudden movement startled Juliette who blinked angrily and immediately went red in the face. Both tiny fists balled furiously and her lips pulled into a grimace. Evie lunged at the table for the water bottle, and at the same time strained to hear what was happening in the next room.

A moment of waiting silence ensued, and then Olivia peered around the doorway, her face pale and her eyes round. "Guess who's here?"

Chapter Five

"Can't you get rid of him?" Evie whispered.

"He asked to see you," Olivia said crossly. "What am I supposed to say?"

Juliette gave one small gasping sob that hinted at impending wails. Both women looked at the baby, then back at each other. Evie wrung her hands and glanced around the kitchen. There was certainly no place to hide. If she tried to slip up the kitchen stairs to Olivia's apartment, he'd see her through the doorway. "Tell him I'm not here," she said desperately.

"Don't be ridiculous. He knows you're here."

The baby's face reddened, and she kicked her tiny, socked feet.

"Oh, Lord," Evie said. "Please, sweetie, don't fuss." She took Juliette out of her swing and started a frantic, bouncing in place. The baby, unappeased, balled one fist against her gums, squeezed her eyes shut and took a prodigious, shuddering breath.

Olivia gave Evie a hard and questioning look. "Well?"

"Can't you tell him I'm sick or something?"

Olivia was suddenly still. "I love you very much, Evie, but I'm not going to tell lies."

"Oh, my God. What am I going to do?"

"Here, hand her to me, and you go talk to him."

"But—but what if he sees her? What if somebody else comes in and you have to go out there?"

"Well, if you can't get rid of him, take him somewhere. Go get coffee. For Pete's sake, do something."

"How do I look?"

"Horrified and guilty as sin."

"Perfect," Evie said, passing the baby to her friend, "just the look I was going for." She wiped her damp hands against her bottom and walked through the doorway. She was sure Adam would be able to hear her heart whamming away at her ribs.

He was standing in front of an antique Welsh dresser, picking absently through a basket of marble eggs.

"Hi," Evie said.

When he turned toward her, his face flashed with a sudden joy that caused something inside her to leap and strain toward him. No one else had ever, or could ever, make her feel that way. The suit he wore was her favorite, a navy blue, double-breasted pinstripe set off with a plain white shirt and gray tie that matched the color of his eyes. He looked tall, handsome and sad. "Hello, gorgeous," he said.

"Liar," she replied, feeling ridiculously pleased.

"I call 'em like I sees 'em."

"Then you need to have your eyes examined," she responded dryly. She didn't want to smile; she just couldn't help it.

Standing motionless, she was aware that he was somehow making a quick, peripheral study of her outline while keeping his piercing gray gaze directed straight into her eyes. His yearning for her, evident in his searching look, surrounded her like an invisible force and urged her toward him. She found it hard to breathe and impossible to think of a thing to say.

The room was silent except for the distant, tinkling music of Olivia's glass wind chimes on the porch. Evie's skin prickled, and everything in the shop seemed to stretch and come to life and train a profound scrutiny on her—listening for nuance and inference, ready to clang an alarm if she should make a wrong move or tell another lie.

Evie, more unsettled with every passing moment, listened for the telltale sound of an infant's cry, and her nerves ratcheted up a notch.

Adam sighed. "How've you been?"

"Okay. Fine." She shifted awkwardly to one foot and had to resist the urge to hug herself, like a guilty child. "Is there . . . have you talked to Tony?"

He made a tiny wince, and the sight of it pierced her. "Yeah," he said. "I brought—" he gestured toward a thick manila envelope lying on one of the cases. "I brought some papers by that we need to go over. It's a questionnaire kind of thing."

Evie glanced at it and then back up at him. She felt an instant loathing for the envelope, and was glad he didn't try to hand it to her. "Okay. Umm, shall I look at it and call you over the weekend? Or maybe Monday?"

Adam looked at her. "Are you busy now? We could sit and talk about...things."

"Well, actually, this isn't the best time. We're kind of busy—"

"I thought you were getting ready to close." Without glancing away, he tipped his shoulder toward the front door. "The sign says you close at five on Friday. Shall I come back later?"

"No!" Evie felt her face reddening. "I mean, it would be better if—if..." Evie heard a slight mewling coming from the kitchen. She knew Adam wouldn't have noticed it yet, because at that moment Juliette's cry was no louder than a kitten's, but Evie knew how quickly the volume and intensity of those cries could escalate.

As a mother she was intimately familiar with every sound her baby made, and she recognized the preamble to a lusty and long-lasting wailing session. *I won't be able stand it—talking to him and listening to her cry. Good grief, what if he wants to see her?* "I—why don't we go for a cup of coffee instead?"

Adam's face lit with unexpected pleasure. "Well, great. Yeah. We should."

"I'll get my purse and tell Olivia. Why don't you go outside and start the car?"

"Oh," his face clouded slightly. "Sure."

Evie grabbed her purse from the kitchen table and a sweater off the back of a chair. "I'll be back in thirty minutes," she whispered, though by then Adam was far out of earshot. "Will you be all right?"

"Go," Olivia said. "Take your time. We'll be fine."

"You're a godsend," Evie said, and ran through the shop and out the front door.

The crisp air held a taste of fall, woodsmoke and the promise of a cold night. Cool, dry weather came rarely to Houston, if at all, and the bite in the air made Evie glad for a chance to be outside. As soon as she reached the end of the porch, she saw that Adam waited in the car with the engine running.

When she opened the door, she heard music playing softly and felt a stab of nostalgia. How many times had she gone running down the steps to jump into a waiting car with Adam? How many times had he been waiting with new, good music to share with her? Since she'd been a child, not even fifteen years old. Of course, in those days he'd treated her just like a little sister—a pet whose company he'd enjoyed.

"Ready?" he asked, and his grin reached his eyes.

"Right," she replied. "But I can't be gone long."

He nodded, and she saw his exuberance fade. "Sure."

As Evie buckled herself in she noticed that the car smelled new; she hadn't been aware of that the first time she'd ridden in it. The interior was plush and beige with the quiet understatement that softens the indicia of extreme success. Evie felt a piercing sadness. As always, her admiration for his accomplishments was blunted by the unspoken question, How much is enough?

"How about Otto's?" he asked. "Since we're this close, I've got to have a plate of ribs."

"I'm not really hungry," she replied. But the image of Otto's barbecue, once evoked, worked its magic. Suddenly she realized she *was* hungry. Starving, in fact. "Well, okay. But like I said, I can't be gone long. Juliette, you know. I don't want to take advantage of Olivia."

She saw him shift slightly. No one else would have noticed it, but she had an intimate knowledge acquired through years of observation—not to mention love. Adam was uncomfortable, but he didn't want it to show.

"We could..."

She saw by his hesitation that he was unsure and searching for words.

He shrugged. "We could bring her with us, if you want."

"No," Evie blurted out. "I—I mean, thanks, but it's a real production to get her ready to go outside. Especially since it's cold today."

The relief evidenced by the sudden easing in his shoulders saddened her beyond words. He didn't seem to notice.

"It is a perfect day, isn't it?" he said. "We don't get many of these."

"No," she murmured. "We don't."

They reached the restaurant in less than ten minutes, and as soon as Evie opened the car door and stepped out into Otto's parking lot, she smelled familiar, wonderful scents—hickory smoke, onions and the countless savory and sinful delights of simple home-style food.

The dining room was fairly quiet, caught between the late lunch crowd and the early dinner rush, and they walked up to the counter almost in step. When he stood aside to let her pass in front of him, he laid a quick, guiding hand to the middle of her back. Even through her clothing, her nerve endings remembered his touch and ignited with a hundred demanding memories. Gooseflesh rose in anticipation. Evie practically jumped forward.

An aluminum handrail, which had been installed to keep Otto's customers in an orderly line during rush hours, contributed to the informal, cafeteria-style atmosphere. Everything else about the fifty-year-old diner, from the plastic condiment bottles to the insurance company calendar at the cash register was also extremely casual. The food, however, was deadly serious: brisket barbecued to melt-in-your-mouth tenderness, thick, juicy ribs; roasted chicken and blazing hot sausages, served, as the wall-size menu promised, "with all the fixins."

"I'll have one of everything," Evie muttered. "With extra bread."

"Pig," Adam said. The word popped out of his mouth with a deep chuckle. "Give me two of everything and a whole pie."

"Double pig."

These were their ritual words and to have left them unsaid would have been overtly rude. Saying them, however, reminded Evie once again of everything that was lost between them—all the private jokes and shared confidences of long-time intimacy.

As Adam studied the menu, Evie once again felt overcome by a wave of nostalgia. Otto's seemed so homey and familiar, like an uncomplicated old friend who never changed. Long ago, before Adam began devoting every weekend to work, Otto's had been one of their "Sunday places." After a lazy morning in bed, reading the paper, drinking coffee and making love, they always ate at one of their favorite, inexpensive restaurants. Otto's had been Evie's first choice and still seemed just the same.

The customary pandemonium and clang of huge pots blasting from the kitchen bounced off the wood-paneled walls and concrete floor. Not one picture in the room hung straight, and the maroon vinyl covering the booths had faded to the color of cheap wine and was liberally patched with silver duct tape. Evie knew the seats were so old they crackled and split if you shifted your weight suddenly.

"You want to take something back to Olivia?" Adam asked. "We could get some sliced brisket or a dinner to go."

"Thanks for offering, but we'd better not," Evie replied. He could be so considerate. When he felt like it. "She's dieting. Watching her cholesterol and fat, you know."

Adam nodded, then tilted his head thoughtfully to the side. "How 'bout baked chicken, no sauce?"

Evie wrinkled her nose. "That would be cruel." A devil was dancing in Adam's eyes, and Evie knew what was coming next. Again, she started to smile without wanting to. He always brought out the mischief in her. As she did in him. She looked up at him and let him see the twinkle in her eye.

"Damn the torpedoes?" he asked.

"Yeah," she replied, with a grin. "Damn the torpedoes."

Adam turned resolutely to the solid-looking woman behind the counter, and she took a ballpoint from behind her ear and gave it an authoritative click. The little badge just over her broad, plaid chest read Nan.

"A pound of sliced beef, a whole chicken and a pint of sauce to go, please. And for here, I'd like a dinner number three, beans and slaw on the side."

She nodded approvingly. Nan evidently liked a customer who knew his mind. "Drink?"

"Draft and glass of water, lots of ice."

Her pen flew across the green pad scrawling her waitress shorthand. She looked at Evie, lifted one brow and held her hand poised, obviously not wanting to break her rhythm.

"Chicken quarter, dark meat," Evie said. "Pickles and potato salad. Large iced tea, please."

Nan nodded. "Coming up." She turned and barked the order to a small, thin man wielding a lethal-looking cleaver. By the time Adam had opened his wallet and passed some bills across the counter, Nan had loaded two trays with their food and drinks, silverware wrapped in napkins and a roll of paper towels— one of Otto's trademark courtesies. "I'll keep your 'to go' back here in the warmer 'til you're ready," she said.

The room was nearly empty, and Evie took the booth that looked out on Otto's patio. Two young men sat at one of the sturdy picnic tables enjoying the brilliant weather and sharing a pitcher of beer and an enormous pile of ribs. Evie watched them for a moment, then turned back to Adam, who'd slid into the seat opposite her. "Thank you for this. It looks fab."

"My pleasure," he said.

Evie knew she needed to broach the uncomfortable subject of the manila envelope, but even the idea of it seemed an ugly intrusion in the warm and congenial atmosphere. "How's work?"

He shrugged. "Same. Busy."

She nodded.

"So tell me," he said as he unwrapped his silverware, "how'd you happen to go to work for Olivia?"

Her daughter is my obstetrician-gynecologist.

"Uh, we—I—just like you said the other day, I always thought the shop looked interesting, and one day I just walked in." Evie trained all her concentration on slowly unfolding her paper napkin and placing it in her lap. She was afraid her face was flaming.

"Oh," Adam said. "Interesting."

She nodded stiffly. Did he sound suspicious? she wondered. *I think he did. He knows something's up.*

"Did Marlene live with you there or somewhere else?"

Oh, my God. Well, at least I knew this was coming.

She looked him straight in the eye. "I can't talk about Marlene, Adam. That's just too painful of a subject for me."

He believed her. She could tell by the softening in his look. At least her answer wasn't a blatant lie. She'd always hated liars and lying. Horrifying, she thought, how quickly you can get good at it.

"I'm sorry," he said. "I didn't mean to—"

"It's okay."

He brightened suddenly. "You'll never guess who I ran into."

"Who?"

"Eddie and Margie."

Evie smiled and a little chuckle tickled the back of her throat. "The Humpsteads?"

He grinned enormously. "You're not going to believe this, but I was with Fred and that's how I introduced them. 'Fred, these are some of my old neighbors, Eddie and Margie *Humpstead.*'"

Evie's mouth dropped open. "You didn't."

He nodded, his eyes alight with amusement at his own faux pas.

When they'd first moved to Houston, Eddie and Margie Hampstead had lived in the town house next door, and their frequent, vigorous and noisily impassioned lovemaking had caused their neighbors to dub them The Humpsteads.

Evie couldn't help but laugh, and the laughter diffused her tension. For the next twenty minutes she even slid back into light conversation about old friends, new music and movies, and the small doings of their mutual acquaintances.

"Have you talked to Louis lately?" she asked.

"The day I got back, but not since then. He's doing great in L.A. Selling his art and getting a tan."

"Who'd have thought it?" Evie murmured. "I'll never forget the two of you with that two-man chain saw cutting cypress knees and making all those hideous coffee tables."

Adam grinned. "Not to mention our tasteful cypress-knee wall clocks." He set down a well-gnawed rib bone and wiped his sauce-reddened fingers. "But you've got your nerve poking fun at our creations, you were part of it, too. As I remember you put down a mean coat of shellac."

"Don't remind me. That's probably why I never became a great artist. I offended the god of good taste."

"That's not true," he said. "You made our house a work of art." He grew suddenly sober. "You should come and see it sometime."

There. It was finally out. Evie had felt the unmentioned breach between them becoming more and more insistent the longer they sat and joked together like any other couple enjoying a dinner. Now at least it had been acknowledged and could be dealt with.

Their laughter died and he leveled his gaze at her. "I miss your things in the house. I miss your touch. I miss you."

"I know," she said. "I miss you, too. But you see, Adam, I missed you even more while we were together. That was worse than this. Now at least I'm not abandoned by you on a daily basis. Now when you don't come home, it's because we don't live together, not because you don't care."

"It was never because I didn't care, Evie. You know that."

"Do I?" she sighed. "Well, maybe that's true. Maybe you did care, you just didn't care enough."

She could see frustration slam through him. Everything about him bristled with it. "Evie, you know how close I am—we are—to achieving the kind of success that'll give us everything we want... all sorts of time together. Every ambitious person has to work a long time getting somewhere. You used to be—"

"Excuse me, Adam. I'm not going to have this conversation again. I know what you tell yourself you're working to accomplish, but you can't see that every time you attain one goal, you set another one even farther away. Farther away from me, too. What you're pursuing is called 'more.' That's all you'll ever want. More. You left me and our marriage to go get more."

"It's not the money—"

"I know that. You're just being you."

"Evangeline," he began, and Evie knew he was on the verge of becoming angry, "if you would just—"

"Adam? Adam Rabalais?" A heavyset, red-faced man appeared just at Evie's shoulder. She hadn't seen him approaching.

"Cal." Adam stood and took the other man's hand. Evie watched silently as Adam greeted his friend without ever letting on that the interruption might be inconvenient. That was Adam's way. Evie was always impressed with all the people he knew—all the names he could remember.

"Great to see you, buddy," Adam said. "Evie," he said turning to her, "This is Cal Dixon. We were in

Dubai at the same time a couple of years ago. Cal, this is my wife, Evie.''

Evie plastered a smile on her face and took the hand he offered. ''Nice to meet you, Mr. Dixon.''

''Please, ma'am, call me Cal,'' he said, pumping her hand with enthusiasm.

Adam stepped to Evie's side of the booth. ''Care to join us?'' he asked, smoothly offering his seat.

Cal, not as tall as Adam but twice as wide, held up both palms. ''Can't. Meetin' some folks in a few minutes.''

''Well then, sit with us until they get here.''

''Now I'll sure do that,'' he said. He looked toward the counter and clapped his hands together with a meaty slap. ''Nan,'' he bellowed.

She looked up and acknowledged him with a disgusted flap of her bar towel. ''What?''

''Somebody bring me a beer?''

She rolled her eyes. ''Like you need one,'' she replied, arching her brows and letting her eyes fall dramatically to his protruding middle. Still, as she turned toward the cooler, Evie saw her mouth curve. Heaving a guffaw, Cal slapped his belly then settled himself into the seat across from Evie.

Adam lowered himself next to Evie and rested his arm on the shelf behind her. Her heart sank. It wasn't that she minded the interruption of their conversation, and she certainly didn't mind Cal Dixon joining them; in fact, she liked his hearty, honest, down-to-earth style, but now Adam was sitting right next to her, his broad chest only inches away and beckoning her, inviting her to curl against him and be held. Adam exuded a magnetic attraction that drew her, the same way she knew she did him. Besides the powerful physical inducement, she also struggled with the force of her memories. She knew what it was like to rest her head against him, to absorb his warmth and feel his smooth skin come alive with her touch.

His long thigh grazed hers, and millions of unseen fibers along her right side awakened and strained toward him. He moved his leg slightly, just enough to hint at a caress. The image of his naked legs flashed in her memory—long, powerful thighs and smoothly muscled calves, tanned and dusted with sun-bleached hair. His strong hips starkly pale against his darker flesh. An awareness curled between her legs. *Do it. Just touch his leg. Nothing more. You know you want to.*

Evie bit her lip and tried to look interested in the conversation. *I have no idea what they're talking about,* she thought. Adam was saying something about a new kind of drilling mud and Cal seemed enraptured by the news. Evie took a drink of tea. Lukewarm. She made a face and set her glass down.

"What's the matter there?" Cal asked.

"Oh, it's nothing. All the ice melted."

Adam's arm fell lightly on her shoulders. "Do you want some more, honey?"

There was nothing she could do. Shrugging his arm off would be rude. Cal would notice, and that would embarrass Adam. Besides, she didn't want to. "No, I'm fine."

"Hup," said Cal, rocking to the side to look toward the door. "There's Willie." He took Adam's hand as he stood. "Don't get up now," he said. "Nice to meet you, ma'am. Call me, Adam. I think we can do business."

He left them and wound through the tables to meet his companion. Adam sat very still, his arm still pressing lightly across her shoulders. Slowly she leaned into him, and he gathered her closer.

"Evie," he murmured. "Sweetheart."

Don't do this. You'll regret it. She reached over and put her arm around him. There had never been a place where she felt as perfectly safe as she did in Adam's arms. His hand grazed her cheek and teased her face upward. When she looked up at him, she saw his eyes filled with determination and passion.

When his mouth first touched hers, a little sigh escaped her. Adam must have taken it as a surrender because his embrace became stronger, more possessive, and yet more tender. He teased her lips apart with his tongue, and she moved her palm to lie flat against his chest. His heart pounded beneath her hand. Her own heart was racing and she felt the heat of months of pent-up desire.

She realized she was starving for him. For his hands on her body. For their bodies to be joined. It didn't matter that they were sitting here in broad daylight. In a restaurant. She reached up to touch his face and felt the late-afternoon roughness on his cheeks. She knew that later on, her face would be ruined from the coarseness. And not just her face. She ran her fingers into his thick hair to hold his face to hers, and he moaned right into her mouth.

And at that moment the phone in his breast pocket rang.

Evie flinched, but fought as she would fight waking up from a beautiful dream. *No! Make it go away.* He pulled away from her and, muttering a curse, reached into his pocket.

"I'm sorry," he murmured hoarsely. "I should have left it in the car. I'll get rid of whoever it is."

The dark gray phone folded neatly over and was no larger than a woman's wallet. Evie wanted to throw it off a cliff.

"Rabalais," Adam said, irritation reddening his already dark skin.

Evie, still breathless, let her hand trail down his torso to the rumpled folds of his trousers where his leg met his hip. Her blood was singing and her mouth tingled with the kisses she'd had and the promise of more to come.

Adam turned to her, his gray eyes intent and full of regret. "Evie, I'm sorry, honey, I've got to take this."

No blast of Arctic air could have made her so suddenly cold. Adam didn't notice because he'd already turned from her and was fumbling for a pen so he could write something on a napkin.

Evie touched him firmly on his shoulder and when he glanced at her she motioned toward the bathrooms. He stood up and she slid across the seat and walked to ladies' room on wobbly legs. As soon as the door closed she let a couple of angry tears slide out. Her reflection in the mirror told the tale.

Skin flushed and radiant, a slight whisker burn glowing on her chin and eyes brimming and betrayed again. "When are you ever going to learn?" she said. She powdered her face, smoothed on wine-colored lipstick and dragged a brush through her hair. A pay phone hung on the wall in the little hallway, so she called Olivia, to check on the baby.

When she walked back toward the table Adam looked up and she could tell he knew she'd been crying. Every stiffened muscle in her body was broadcasting her anger and disgust with herself.

He stood aside to offer her the seat she'd had next to him. She made a deliberate point of going to the other side of the booth. There, wedged into the corner was the manila envelope, and she picked it up and put it on the table between them.

"Now," she said, "tell me about this."

HOW TO VALIDATE
YOUR
EDITOR'S FREE GIFT
"THANK YOU"

1. Peel off gift seal from front cover. Place it in space provided at right. This automatically entitles you to receive four free books and a Cuddly Teddy Bear.

2. Send back this card and you'll get brand-new Silhouette Romance™ novels. These books have a cover price of $3.25 each, but they are yours to keep absolutely free.

3. There's no catch. You're under no obligation to buy anything. We charge nothing — ZERO — for your first shipment. And you don't have to make any minimum number of purchases — not even one!

4. The fact is thousands of readers enjoy receiving books by mail from the Silhouette Reader Service™ months before they're available in stores. They like the convenience of home delivery and they love our discount prices!

5. We hope that after receiving your free books you'll want to remain a subscriber. But the choice is yours — to continue or cancel, anytime at all! So why not take us up on our invitation, with no risk of any kind. You'll be glad you did!

6. Don't forget to detach your FREE BOOKMARK. And remember…just for validating your Editor's Free Gift Offer, we'll send you FIVE MORE gifts, *ABSOLUTELY FREE!*

GET A FREE TEDDY BEAR…

*You'll love this plush, Cuddly Teddy Bear, an adorable accessory for your dressing table, bookcase or desk. Measuring 5½" tall, he's soft and brown and has a bright red ribbon around his neck — he's completely captivating! And he's yours **absolutely free,** when you accept this no-risk offer!*

Chapter Six

"Are you sure I can't get you anything?" Olivia asked.

"No, thanks," Evie replied. "We've got everything we need for right now, and I plan to do a big grocery shop later in the week." She sighed and pressed her hands into the small of her back. "I'm just so tired all the time. Ever since the baby came I don't have any energy. It seems like the minute I wake up I'm looking forward to going to bed. You've had kids, Livvie, when do you stop being tired?"

Olivia gave her a little smile. "Well, if I remember correctly, that clears up just as soon as they leave for college."

Evie rolled her eyes. "Oh, great. Just eighteen years to go."

Olivia laughed gently. "I'm sorry," she said, "I shouldn't joke about it. Once she sleeps through the night you'll feel better. I know this sounds crazy, but try to enjoy this part. You'd be surprised how fast it goes by and how much you'll miss it." She checked her watch. "Well," she said, "I need to fly if I'm going to make the deposit before the bank closes." Her eyes sparkled. "I believe we're going to have our best month ever, and it's not even Christmas season yet."

Evie smiled wistfully. "Things are really picking up, aren't they?" She was glad for her friend, but since she planned to leave soon, she knew she wouldn't be able to share in the success she'd helped to bring about. The thought of leaving left her suddenly bereft. Lately it seemed that all she did was say goodbye to people she loved.

Olivia obviously caught the melancholy tone in her voice, because she gave her a look of regret tinged with reproach. "You know I wish more than anything that you'd stay. Having the two of you here has made me happier than I've been in years. It's wonderful to have a baby in the house again."

"I wish there was a way I could. I don't know what we would have done without you, but I'm afraid if I stay, Adam will see her. He told me he's going back to South America in a couple of weeks, but he said he'll be coming back to Houston at least once a quarter. Maybe more. You've seen how he is. He'll just show up any time he feels like it, and you know what that means."

"Have you spoken with him since last week?"

Evie shook her head. "No. He called on Sunday, but I was screening my calls and I didn't pick up. He left some ridiculous message, saying he had a question about stocks for the final property settlement, but I'm sure it was just an excuse to get me on the phone to wear me down. The petition was filed yesterday, and he's signed a waiver for his appearance, so I can get—I mean I can go down to the courthouse with Tony in sixty days and have it finalized without Adam even showing up."

Talking about the divorce papers gave her a sick feeling. One of the paragraphs said that there were "no children of the marriage and none expected." Remembering how she had signed and sworn to a lie of that magnitude filled her with a sense of dread, but she forced the emotion down. That was done and over, all in the past. Now she'd never have to think about it again. But talking about the ending of her marriage made her miserable.

Evie had been sorting and labeling a shipment of Thai baskets that had come in that morning, and she picked up another one and tied a little price tag on it. Staying busy usually helped her feel better, but today nothing seemed to sooth the feeling of seasick misery in her middle. "I told him not to call me anymore, and to just have Tony mail me the property settlement papers when they were ready. I know he'll be fair. No matter what else he is, Adam is one of the most honest people I've ever met. So you see, there's really no reason for me to ever talk to him again."

Her eyes were now swimming and she didn't dare look up at Olivia. "Besides, I just can't talk to him.

And I certainly can't see him. I couldn't take another scene like we had at Otto's.''

Olivia's mouth flattened with disgust. "I could just pinch his head off. And after the way he acted here in the shop, too—like he'd do just about anything to have you back. What on earth got into him?''

Evie shrugged. "That's just Adam. First things first.'' Although this was Wednesday, almost a week later, thinking about the way he'd treated her— brushing her off casually in a moment of intimacy just to take a phone call—still made her chest tight with humiliation and outrage. He'd tried to smooth it over by saying the call was some emergency or other, but Evie had told him to save it, she wasn't interested in any more excuses. Not ever.

She couldn't stand remembering their disastrous dinner. The way she'd practically swooned in his arms filled her with disgust at herself, all the more because she knew she was likely to do exactly the same thing again if they were alone together. She had no will-power when it came to Adam. She'd been in love with him more than half her life.

She still was.

She knew the only way to guarantee there wouldn't be a repeat of Friday's incident was to avoid him al-together. Juliette had to be her first consideration, and that meant staying away from Adam. She just couldn't let her personal weakness entice her back into an-other situation like the one at the restaurant.

Evie's tears were still burning the back of her throat when Juliette chose to embark on one of her strange, spontaneous vocal exercises. Lately, the sound of her own voice seemed to both fascinate and surprise her. She would make sudden, musical jungle cries, then look startled and astonished.

She lay in her carrier in the center of the table, cooing and drumming the air with clumsy strokes as if she were conducting an unseen orchestra. Every day there were more changes. She was growing like a weed, smiling some, grabbing her pink toes and focusing her intent gray gaze on the world that was slowly unfolding for her. Sometimes Evie felt the most piercing sadness, knowing that Adam would never share the staggering sense of awe she felt when she held this new life—a creation made from part of each of them.

"When I get back why don't we have a cup of tea outside?" Olivia gently suggested. "It's a shame to waste these gorgeous evenings."

"Let's do that," Evie said. "While you're gone, I'll feed Little Miss Priss and finish the inventory."

Olivia began gathering her things, but just as she was headed for the door the shop phone rang. Closing time had passed, so both women waited for the answering machine to get the call. The recorded message cycled, and then Adam's voice, clipped and harsh, filled the kitchen.

"Evie, it's Adam. Maybe you didn't get the message I left for you on Sunday. If you really expect to get these papers finished before I leave for South America, I need to ask you a couple of questions. I'll be here at the office until at least ten." He didn't bother to say goodbye before he hung up, but he did make a point of leaving his phone number. Evie knew that was meant as a particularly sarcastic gesture. His office number hadn't changed in years.

After he hung up, the mechanical, monotone voice of the machine droned the time. Evie screwed her face into a grimace at the machine and mimicked Adam's voice. "If you really expect to get these papers finished, I expect you to blah, blah, blah. Oh, spare me."

Olivia's eyebrows rose. "Well, he sounded *very* cross."

"No, he didn't," Evie said. "He's just so frustrated he can't stand it. He *hates* not getting his way."

"Are you sure? I thought he sounded like he was ready to come through the phone."

Evie pointed her finger and hit the Erase button on the recorder with a satisfied flourish. The tape squealed as it rewound and obliterated the message. "I've only seen Adam really lose his temper one time, and that's not the way he acted." She glanced at her friend. "Do you have time for this before you go? You do? Okay. Well, we'd been married for about two years when I graduated from LSU. Every year the Fine Arts Department had a graduation party in one of the big studios, and that year somebody's drunken friend showed up with a couple of his fraternity brothers. At first they were pretty easy to ignore—just obnoxious fraternity jerks.

"But as the evening wore on they got a lot worse for wear and started roughhousing. You know, making lewd comments about the figure drawings and acting like they were going to pick up a bust or piece of sculpture and start playing football. Anyway, my back was turned, and one of them knocked me into a set of metal greenware shelves.

"I chipped my tooth and bit my lip and started bleeding all over the place. Well, as you can imagine, there was chaos for a couple of minutes, everybody running around like chickens trying to get something to wrap some ice in. I was crying, and the guy was upset but still trying to be funny—you know, making jokes, and that's when Adam appeared out of nowhere. He'd been off by himself looking at the exhibits.

"When he walked in everybody in the room just froze, and I got the most sickening feeling that something really horrible was getting ready to happen. My face was pretty well mopped up by then but still bleeding a little, and my dress was ruined. When Adam saw what had happened, he went completely still. He just froze in place—strangest thing I ever saw. He even stopped blinking. It was like he went into some sort of trance. For a minute nobody breathed, and then he looked over at the guy, and I swear he was almost smiling. Anyway, in this really spooky voice he said, 'Get him out of here.'

"Well, I've never seen a drunk sober up so fast in my life. I hear they drove him all the way back to Shreveport that night." Evie shrugged. "When we got home I asked Adam why he acted like that, and he told me he always got that way when he was really afraid. I said, 'You were afraid of a couple of loaded fraternity baboons?' and he said, 'No. I was afraid I was going to kill him.'" Evie didn't smile. "He meant it, too."

She looked up at her friend. "And that's what Adam's like when he's *really* mad." With a flap of her hand she dismissed the message he'd left on the answering machine. "That's just him blowing off steam because he's not getting his way. Adam Rabalais is the most stubborn, obstinate human being I've ever met."

Before Olivia turned away, she gave Evie a skeptical look. "I wonder if he'd agree with you," she murmured.

Evie didn't reply.

Hours later Olivia still hadn't returned, so Evie took Juliette out on the deck to enjoy the sunset. The air was sweetly perfumed with the scents of freshly mown grass, star jasmine and late-blooming gardenias. Monkey grass defined the curving borders of the perfectly tended lawn, and magnolias, Chinese cherry trees and flowering shrubs shaded the beds. Although Evie admired Olivia's yard and enjoyed working with her in it, she often missed her own garden, and every time she remembered it, she felt as if she'd abandoned a friend.

Evie tried not to think about it and to enjoy the quiet moment. This was her favorite time of year; the long, cool evenings of Indian summer. The year's first cold front had spent itself within a day or so, and she was glad the evening was warm enough to bring Juliette's carrier outside. Sitting on the deck in the fading light, Evie was struck by the thought that everything was coming to an end—the summer, the brief island of quiet she'd spent living with Olivia.

And her marriage to Adam.

The leaves on Olivia's ash tree had turned from glossy green to pale yellow as the drowsy tree slowly went to sleep for the winter. That evening the quiet, golden air was filled with the tumble of dying leaves, the sigh of the fading summer and the silent fall tears.

Adam turned down Westheimer for the third time that night. The digital clock on the instrument panel showed that it was after ten. That meant he'd been driving back and forth in front of her house for more than an hour. The lights in Evie's apartment were still on, and he once again had the same argument with himself. *Just go up there, knock on the door and make her talk to you. She's got to talk to you sometime.*

No, leave it alone. She probably won't let you in, anyway. Wait until tomorrow.

But I'm running out of time. I have to leave in a week. I've already been gone from the plant too long.

Look, here's the driveway. You're going to pass it. Damn. You should have turned in.

He tightened his fingers around the leather-covered steering wheel until his knuckles ached. When he'd stormed out of the office more than an hour ago, he'd intended to drive over, march straight up to her door and demand that she talk to him. He knew she was still mad about last Friday.

Once again, Evie had overreacted about one of his business commitments and had completely lost her temper. He knew she was screening her calls and refusing to speak to him. This was just the kind of childish ploy that had become her trademark in the past year.

But the closer he came to where she lived, the more he doubted himself. And once he reached the shop, instead of pounding up the stairs and hammering on her door like he'd envisioned, he just drove aimlessly up and down her street, taking ridiculous comfort from the sight of the light in her window.

"Well, this has got to be one of your finest moments, so I sure hope you're proud of yourself," he said in disgust as he drove past again. "I think this officially qualifies you as a stalker." He shook his head. "You're being stupid," he muttered. *Go home. Leave her alone for now and go try to get some sleep.*

He groaned and shoved a hand through his hair. Every muscle in his body screamed with fatigue, and he'd become snappish and short-tempered at work because he was so damn tired. Now he was lucky if he got a couple of hours of uninterrupted sleep a night. It was those damn dreams. They were getting worse all the time.

Lately, a new and more disturbing element had appeared in his nightmares. Now, he'd inexplicably begun to hear a baby crying—wailing with inconsolable heartache and desolation. The crying unnerved him because he didn't know what it meant. Could it be the crying of his unborn children, he wondered? Children he would never have if Evie left him. He knew there would never be anyone else for him if she went through with the divorce. Maybe it was supposed to be Marlene Hitchcock's baby crying, he thought. Adam felt a stab of guilt about that.

Tony hadn't been able to find out anything about the woman, and Adam wished more than ever that some outraged family member would appear and claim the child. Maybe even threaten some kind of legal action—anything to get Evie to come to him—to need him again. The part about the baby was sad, though. Poor little thing, he thought. Rotten luck for a kid. Not to have real parents.

Just like Evie.

Still, he didn't have much sympathy to spare for anyone else; he was desperate with exhaustion. He hated his dreams and dreaded going to bed. It was horrible to lie there at night aching for sleep and to have his head echo with that terrible crying and, no matter how hard he tried, to be unable to figure out what it meant.

When he reached Interstate 10, he turned east, and his windshield was immediately alight with the jagged downtown skyline spangled with thousands of illuminated office windows. He could see One Shell Plaza, easily recognizable by the enormous antenna on top, and toyed for a moment with the idea of going back to the office, but when he reached the Studemont exit he turned south and headed home toward his empty house.

Evie sat on the little overstuffed love seat and looked through a box of old photographs. She'd been sitting there for more than an hour, legs curled beneath her and the lamp drawn up close so she could see better. She wore her favorite outfit, thick socks, warm cotton leggings and one of Adam's cast-off, oversize sweaters. This one had once been beige, but had long since faded to the color of oatmeal. It was cable knit and nubby with age and swallowed her completely.

She blamed her latest fit of nostalgia on the sweater. When she'd lived with Adam and he was out of town, she would often put on his clothes to wrap herself in the suggestion of his presence. Tonight, after she'd come in and put the baby down, she'd tried to watch television, but had wound up pulling out the pictures instead.

Months ago, when she'd left their house for the last time, she'd felt guilty about taking the photographs with her. Later on she'd convinced herself Adam would probably never notice they were gone. With a bitter shrug she'd told herself he would probably hardly notice that she was gone, either.

The floor around her was littered with photos, the lights low and the baby long asleep when she heard the first noise. Was that a car, she wondered, engine killed, gliding into the driveway? She put down the picture and listened intently. Although everything seemed quiet, and she wasn't really sure she'd even heard anything, she still sat up—alert and barely breathing. Then she heard the unmistakable creak of footsteps coming quietly up the outside stairs followed by a knock so faint, she wondered if it was meant to be heard.

Gooseflesh rose on her spine. It was nearly eleven. Who would come by this late? What if it was a prowler? She unfolded her legs, slid from the couch and slipped quietly over to the door. On the way she picked up the phone and clutched it to her chest, poised to dial the emergency code if need be. "Who's there?"

"It's me, Evie. Adam."

Great jumping Jehosaphat.

"I'm asleep, Adam," she said, trying to sound groggy.

"No you're not," he said.

Evie stood behind the door stupefied with fright and at a total loss for words.

"You can open the door now or I can start banging on it," Adam said conversationally.

"You'll wake the baby," she said, low and urgently.

"Yes," he replied. "I will."

"Come back tomorrow," she said.

A moment of silence followed, and Evie listened hopefully for the sound of masculine footsteps retreating back down the stairs. Instead, two hard, loud raps rattled the door. During the day the racket would have been intrusive, but in the middle of the quiet night it echoed like two minor explosions. A dog started yammering in the next yard.

Evie immediately unlocked the door as quietly as she could and stood glaring up at him. "What?" she asked furiously.

Uninvited, Adam stepped by her, and his gaze immediately fell to the photographs spread on the couch and tumbling onto the floor. He eyed Evie. "I wondered what happened to those."

Evie, scarlet with guilt and frantic with apprehension, stood by the door and hugged herself. "What are

you doing here? It's late. I have to go to work tomorrow."

"Yeah," he said. "So do I."

"Adam," she said through clenched teeth, but he
was already kneeling on the floor, his back turned to
her.

*Oh, my God, are there any of me pregnant? No,
they're in the baby book. Please be in the baby book.*

Adam was ignoring her, and for a moment she
stared at his back, then she resigned herself to the visit
and hoped that the damned dog next door would quiet
down before Juliette woke up and all hell broke loose.
Thank God, she thought, after another indignant bark
or two, the animal woofed into silence.

Evie locked the door, sat down in the rocking chair
and watched Adam do exactly what she had been doing moments earlier. Although a smile flickered
around his mouth, she thought he looked tired. Hag-
gard, in fact. Probably working too hard, she told
herself.

"Look," he said, and held up a snapshot. "You and
me at the Alexanders' with Snoopy." His voice was
hushed. "You were what? Sixteen?"

"Seventeen," she replied. She'd almost cried over
the photograph an hour ago. "I was selling pony rides
to get money for. . . something."

He looked up at her. "My birthday," he said. "You
bought me a leather jacket."

She nodded. Even though at the time they were only
friends, at least as far as Adam was concerned, they'd
still bought each other extravagant gifts. She'd been
crazy about him, and he'd spoiled her rotten.

"Adam," she said, feeling the beginnings of helpless desperation. "It's really late and I've got to go to bed. Actually I was just headed that way."

"Yeah," he said without looking up. "I can see that." One by one he picked up the old photographs and sighed or smiled or shook his head, then put them back in the stacks Evie had been making. For a few moments she tried to resist the urge to look over his shoulder. In the end she couldn't and instead joined him on the floor—careful not to sit too close—and took extraordinary care to be the one to take the photographs from the box so she could keep a watchful eye for photos of her with a conspicuously bulging middle.

"Oh, man," he said in a voice reminiscent of teen-aged enthusiasm. "The 'stang."

Evie took the photograph from him. The two of them stood next to the red Mustang convertible Adam had bought when he turned twenty-one. Evie was nearly seventeen and he'd taught her to drive in that car.

And to kiss. But that was a year later.

Evie couldn't help but smile. They'd probably still have it, but Adam got so many speeding tickets driving between LSU and Evansville, he eventually had to sell it or risk losing his driver's license for good. They'd even given the car a going away party.

"Oh, here's one," he said flatly. "Uncle Cuckoo and Aunt Marble Heart."

Evie scowled, irritated that he used the nicknames he'd made up for her aunt and uncle. She took the picture from him. Richard Delaney looked exactly like what he was—a math and physics genius with an IQ off the scale and a temperament uniquely unsuited for a role as involuntary foster parent. He wore his customary shocked-owl expression along with tartan plaid shorts and a striped shirt, pale blue socks, brown sandals and thick, black-rimmed bifocals.

Next to him, and slightly taller than her husband, stood Evie's Aunt Nila wearing a gray tailored suit and looking cool and shrewd, which, of course, she was.

Adam sat back, stretched his long legs out and shuffled slowly through one of Evie's carefully sorted stacks.

"Remember this day?" he asked, and rubbed his thumb slowly over the picture he held.

Evie scooted fractionally closer and looked over his shoulder. "How could I forget? That's the day Mary Margaret and I graduated from high school. We had that huge party at the Alexanders."

He turned toward her, his mouth slightly curved with amusement. "And that's not all."

Evie felt a blush rising. That was also the day Adam finally noticed that she'd grown up. She was eighteen, then, and he'd kissed her on the mouth for the first time as she'd stood in the Alexanders' kitchen.

Adam turned toward her. "You were washing dishes because they ran out of silverware."

She grinned. "There must have been a hundred and fifty people there."

"I just remember one," he said.

Evie was lost in the memory. Her back had been to the door, and so many people were coming and going through the kitchen she paid no attention when she heard someone rattling through an ice chest behind her. Her hair was piled on her head because of the heat, but spiral tendrils hung at her nape and temples. She wore crisp, white shorts that showed off her pretty legs and, of course, one of Adam's football jerseys.

She finally turned around, when she realized that whoever had come into the kitchen wasn't leaving. Her nape was prickling from the feeling of being stared at, and when she turned around she saw that it was him. And then she saw the look in his eyes and she knew immediately. He did, too.

For a long moment they stood there, eyes locked in a moment of realization. Then he opened his arms and she walked into them and he kissed her. Even now, so many years later, that day and that kiss remained the most romantic moment in Evie's life.

She became aware of a waiting silence in the room. Once again, just like on the day in the picture, she felt her skin prickling under his gaze.

"That was a kiss," he said softly.

"That was *the* kiss," she replied.

She was so close to him that when he turned to face her she could see the burrs of silver and gray in his eyes. The back of his hand grazed her cheek, and then his fingers cupped her chin as he ran his thumb over her lips. "You still have the prettiest mouth I've ever seen."

Evie knew she couldn't trust her voice. She didn't trust herself. The tip of her tongue grazed his thumb. Salty. Warm.

Then she was in his arms, crushed to his chest with his mouth slanted over hers, devouring her with kisses. He pulled her into his lap as easily as if she'd been a doll, and the realization of his overwhelming strength flashed through Evie's mind. It occurred to her that she wouldn't be able to struggle away. She was glad she didn't want to.

She wrapped her arms around him and pressed her body to his. Everything in her ached for him, and he pulled her back close against his body, touching and searching with his hands and mouth. She rolled her head back, and he trailed kisses down her neck and with one smooth motion laid her down on her back on the hooked rug and cushioned her head with his arm.

One long leg was angled between hers, and she felt, as she was certain he meant her to, the insistent burden between his legs heavy against her thigh. His body, poised over hers, radiated heat and desire, and his right hand teased her sweater up. She sighed when she felt his palm caress her ribs and move up to her breast. His eyes closed and he moaned into her mouth, and teased her lips apart with his tongue.

Then his hand slid back to grasp the back of her knee and urge her to curve her leg around him. She did, arching into him, and he moved his hips against hers. Her blood was roaring through her body, and she needed to feel skin against skin. Pulling his shirt out of his pants, she dragged it against his damp flesh.

His mouth was hot against her neck, and he grabbed the hem of the sweater. "This is mine," he said. "I think I'd like to have it back, please. Now."

He lifted her easily, and she rocked forward to let him pull it up and off her body.

And then she heard Juliette cry.

Evie went rigid with panic. "Stop. Stop. The baby. I have to go. You have to go," she whispered frantically.

She looked up into impassioned, adamant eyes. He caught a quick breath. "No, Evie. I'm going to wait for you."

"You can't. I . . . I don't know how long I'll be with her."

"Where's the coffee?"

The decision was made. She had to go and see to Juliette. "Second shelf," she said, listening for another sob from the baby's room and yanking her clothing back into place. "In the cabinet by the stove." She had one minute to make this sound convincing. "Look, I'd ask you to come see her, but she won't go back to sleep if you do. Strangers make her . . . nervous."

She stood and fled to the baby's room, leaving Adam to sit on the floor resting his head in his palms and his elbows on his knees. He wasn't sure he could stand. He was positive that walking would be painful. His blood was singing in his veins and there was a throbbing, demanding bulge between his legs. He sighed, forced himself to stand and walked through the arched doorway at the opposite end of the room.

He didn't bother to turn on the overhead light; the little stove lamp was plenty to see by. Besides, he didn't want to disturb the quiet of the semidark kitchen. He found the coffee just where she said it would be, filled the kettle at the sink and turned on the stove. There was a hiss of gas, and then a blue flame raced around the burner with a homey, pleasant whoosh. Adam liked the kitchen. It was neat as a pin, scrubbed and organized but somehow managed to radiate Evie's personality.

Photographs, articles and other pieces of curling paper were slapped against the refrigerator and held there by colorful magnets. Pushed against the far wall he saw a linoleum kitchen table with steel tube legs and felt an aching déjà vu. The table was identical to the one in the garage apartment they'd rented while he was in grad school. A set of Evie's antique salt and pepper shakers—the pink cows—was centered on one of the ceramic trivets she'd made in pottery class. Adam picked up the salt cellar, then he noticed the antique folding high chair collapsed neatly out of sight on the other side of the table. He put the shaker back and turned away.

A window over the chipped porcelain sink looked down into Olivia's backyard, and the lights she'd hung in her trees filtered down through the branches and dropped circles of friendly light on the deck and her pretty garden. He was standing at the window, lost in thought and listening to the kettle beginning to rumble when he first heard the baby crying. He straightened up—suddenly alert. Something about the crying was vaguely disturbing.

I know that sound, he thought, and deep within him something twisted and made an ache in his middle. He recognized the crying, although he'd only heard it in his dreams—his terrible dreams of a baby wailing in hopeless desolation.

He moved the kettle from the burner, turned off the gas and walked back through Evie's living room and into the narrow hallway. He walked quietly so she didn't hear him, and when he pushed the door open she didn't see him because her back was turned. She was leaning over and speaking in a quiet but urgent whisper to the baby who lay on her back in a pool of muted light.

Adam looked into Juliette's face and saw his father's eyes, eyes just like his own, staring unblinking at him from a face identical to Evangeline's.

And at last he understood.

Chapter Seven

Evie felt rather than heard Adam come into the room. A sixth sense told her to turn around, and when she did, she saw his face and felt a chill slide up her spine. He stared at her with wide, unblinking eyes.

"What have you done?"

Her mouth fell open but no words came out.

He took a step toward her, and for the first time in her life, Evie felt afraid of him.

"What have you done?" he repeated.

"I—I don't know what you mean." The look on his face never changed, but a surge of contempt rolled from him in a wave. She wanted to look away but couldn't, so instead she raised her chin defiantly. "I did what I had to do."

"This is my baby," he said. His chest rose and fell

as if he couldn't catch his breath. "We have a baby."
And again. "We have a baby."

Emotions crossed his face so rapidly, Evie could
only guess what he felt—incredulity, wonder, a moment of piercing joy. Then his jaw clamped tight and
his eyes turned to slate.

"You lied." His voice was incredulous and outraged. "You made all that up." Then his tone became
eerily quiet. "You wanted to hide my child from me."

A sudden, fearless calm overtook her. "Yes," she
said. "I did."

"Why? How could you do this?" An almost imperceptible movement of his body summed it all up—
to leave him, to hide her pregnancy, to lie about Juliette and try to take her away. "How could you take
this from me?"

"Because," she replied coldly. "You didn't want
her. You said having children would ruin your life.
You said if I got pregnant you would never forgive me,
so I hardly see what you're so—"

His white face flashed suddenly red. "Shut up," he
snapped.

Evie flinched. He'd never spoken to her that way
before, and the words hit her like a slap.

"You're lying," he said. "I never said anything like
that."

Evie's temper engaged and she had to physically re-
strain herself from pointing her finger right in his face.
"Yes." Her jaw was so tightly clenched each word
cracked like a shot. "Yes . . . you . . . did." She sucked
in a furious breath. "Do you want to know the exact
day you said it? Remember after Christmas after the
robbery, when you left me?"

At the mention of that incident, his gaze faltered and her words rushed out, carried on the tide of her anger. "You just had to go to Mexico, remember? And then you just had to go on to San Asfallia to talk to them about the job. If you remember, it was the seventh of January. I called you from the doctor's office right after he told me I was pregnant. That was also the day they offered you the job. I know you remember *that* call."

Adam's brow creased, and she knew he was beginning to recall their conversation.

"And then I said, 'But if it's for three years, we'll have to put off starting a family again. And what happens if I accidentally get pregnant?' And then you said, 'Don't you ruin this for me, Evie. If you do, I won't forgive you.' Remember?"

His jaw went hard again. "That's a pathetic excuse. You should have told me."

"Hah! And let you tell your child she'd ruined your life? Do you really think I would stand aside and watch you break her heart because she caused a hitch in your precious career? Not a chance. Richard used to say that to me all the time. 'You ruined everything. I'll never forgive you for it.' No one is going to say things like that to my baby."

Adam's fists clenched. "How dare you?" he said. "How dare you compare me with that lunatic?"

"Because," she replied, "you said exactly the same things to me that he did."

Apparently Adam had no answer to that, and they glared at each other, Evie blocking the way to the crib, and Adam blocking the way to the door.

Juliette, ignored and obviously feeling the tension in the room, yowled in protest, and Evie immediately turned and gathered her into her blanket and picked her up. "See what you've done?" she flung over her shoulder.

"Oh, don't be—" but he didn't finish. Instead his breath began to slow. "I want to see her. Come into the light."

Evie reluctantly followed him back into the living room, and Juliette snuffled into a tremulous silence, nuzzling against her mother's shoulder. In the center of the room Evie turned, but stayed away from the lamp so the light wouldn't shine directly in the baby's eyes.

Adam stood next to her and reached up to touch the baby's cheek with the back of his fingers; she turned her face toward him. "She's beautiful, isn't she?"

Evie nodded. "Yes."

"Give her to me."

Evie hesitated for an instant, but then a sudden calm overtook her. No matter what else had gone before, or what terrible things were to come, at that moment giving Adam his daughter to hold was the right thing to do. She could see that his entire conscious being was absorbed in that moment, and as she laid Juliette in his arms, she felt something profound happening to all of them.

Evie knew for centuries women had been placing firstborn children into the arms of their fathers, even though those fathers usually had months to anticipate the moment. But as soon as the baby was cradled in his arms, Adam and Juliette locked eyes. Evie knew it was impossible, but it seemed that some silent communication was passing between them—that in that one instant they established a bond that she thought took months of tender nurturing to establish. She felt profoundly overwhelmed and vaguely left out.

"How old is she?"

"Three months."

"So, she was born . . . ?"

"July seventeenth."

His mouth fell open. "Like my mom."

Evie nodded, but he wasn't paying attention to her.

"Is everything . . . okay with her?"

"She's perfect," Evie replied. Speaking had become suddenly difficult. Seeing them together moved her beyond words, beyond tears.

"And you?" he asked, but without looking at her. "Are you all right?"

"Fine."

"I have a lot of questions."

"I'm sure."

She saw in his face that he was as awestruck as she had been the first time she'd touched the baby's palm and had the tiny fingers close around her finger. He was lost as she had been in the perfect flower of her mouth, her flawless skin and the mass of ringlets covering her head. Because she was seeing that same realization in him, Evie again felt the specific pride only a parent can feel in the gift of creation.

Although a terrible conflict now lay between Adam and her, she could see that he felt just as she had the first time she'd held her child in her arms—overwhelmed, humbled and honored. She wondered if he, too, felt a connection to the future and to the past when he held their child. She wished she could ask him, but didn't dare.

He took a slow, quiet breath. "I still can't believe what you did."

His accusation shattered the reverence of the moment. "Well," she said, "I guess I'll just have to learn to live with that."

His eyes snapped toward her. "You'll be moving back into the house then," he said. His words weren't a question, but rather a command.

"I don't think so," she replied. "My plans haven't changed. I'm taking her back to Evansville with me."

The look he gave her was indescribable, but she stepped backward and almost raised her hands in defense.

"I don't think so." His voice was quiet but frightening.

"You can't stop me, Adam," she said.

"I think I can."

"How? You won't even be here, remember? You're going back to South America next week, right? You'll be gone for up to two more years, isn't that right? And where you're going, you can't take small children."

His face hardened into a cold mask, and his voice sounded as if he were dictating a memo to a not-so-bright underling. There was hardly any inflection at all. "You will pack up your personal things and be ready to move back to our house on Sunday morning. I'll arrange to have movers come to get your furniture by noon. You will not try to hide my daughter from me again, and you will not refuse to allow the movers into this apartment. I don't guess I need to re-

mind you that when you filed for divorce recently you
swore to a false affidavit.''

He met her eyes with a cold, satisfied smile. ''I
know the School of Fine Arts didn't require courses in
the law, but I'm sure the word *perjury* rings a bell even
with you. I see it does.''

He took a deep breath, and for the first time in her
life Evie could see how his business adversaries could
fear him. She had never had his ruthlessness directed
at her before. ''And I hope you don't try to remove my
child from the State of Texas, Evangeline, because if
you do, I will slap a restraining order on you so fast
you'll get whiplash. Do you understand me? Good.''

Seeing the coldness in him and knowing he fully intended to force her to move back into their house filled
her with helpless rage. ''I'm still going to divorce you,
Adam. I don't think you can get custody of her. After
all, you won't even be in the country. We both know
what's really important to you, don't we? Your career
comes first. It always has.''

She could see him fighting for control. ''You might
reconsider your disdain for the life I've been trying to
build for the past eight years. Just what the hell do you
think has been supporting you since you were twenty
years old?''

His eyes were full of accusation. ''Have you ever
stopped to wonder why you have such contempt for
money, Evie? It's because there was always plenty to
go around in your family. Richard and Nila always
took care of you, and then we got married and I made
your living. And you've never given me a moment's
credit for that.''

''That's a lie. You know it is.''

He looked her dead in the eye. "Do I? And another thing, don't ever try to bluff me again. You don't have any experience at it. And I guarantee you, if you cross me, I'll file for custody of my daughter and I will get it."

Evie felt a tremor. Could he? Could he take her? "Courts don't give babies to absentee fathers."

"What do you know? Fathers get custody a lot more than you think. And just who do you think a judge would trust? A perjurer? Someone who falsified court documents, hid a child from her father and tried to steal her? Or someone like me who's worked hard, been honest and tried to save his marriage?"

Evie slowly realized the magnitude of her foolishness and extent of her vulnerability. She was utterly helpless to stop him from doing what he threatened.

"And as far as the refinery," he said, "I'll make whatever arrangements are necessary to do my job and still raise my child."

"*Our* child," Evie countered, but her voice lacked conviction. She was drowning in fear. He could do it. He would do it. She let her shoulders fall. "All right. I'll move back into the house."

"And you'll call your family tomorrow and our friends and tell them what you did."

Her temper flashed again. "You can't make me do that."

He smiled humorlessly. "No, I can't. But believe me, Evangeline, you'll be much happier if you're the one who explains what you did and why you did it."

She swallowed. "What about your parents?"

He looked away, and Evie could see the hurt again. "I'll take care of that," he said. "I'd also appreciate it if you'd wear your wedding rings. After all, I did work two jobs for nearly ten months to get you the ones you wanted."

Evie looked down. "I sold them," she said quietly. For a long time he said nothing and when she looked up again, she couldn't discern the emotion in his face. He looked more thoughtful than anything.

"To pay your hospital bills," he said. It wasn't a question.

She nodded. "I didn't want to use the insurance because the bills would go to your office, and I knew you'd—"

"Enough!" he snapped. He turned back to the baby, who murmured and blinked and then gave a prodigious yawn.

Evie hugged herself tightly. "When do you think— Are you still going back to San Asfallia?"

"I'll let you know, but that's not your concern right now. Just be ready to move home by Sunday."

Evie clenched her fists. She might have to do what he said, but didn't have to endure his condescension. "You know, Adam, just because I'm moving back into the house doesn't mean I'm moving back into our room."

He nailed her with a cold look. "Don't flatter yourself, Evie. What makes you think I'd want you to?"

There was nothing more to say. Oddly, in the midst of the bitter and heated conversation, Juliette lay quiet and content in Adam's arms. Once again he looked down into her face, and Evie felt a pang.

Under other circumstances she would have put her arms around him so the three of them could share an embrace. But that would certainly never happen now. The betrayals and resentments that had gone before would separate them with a wall of mistrust neither of them could overcome—even if either of them cared to try. And Juliette, innocent of all of it, would be caught in the middle.

Since there was nothing more to be said, Evie stood and waited for him to decide to leave. However, instead of handing the baby back to her to put to bed, he carried Juliette into her room himself and laid her gently in her crib where she drifted sweetly to sleep. Evie watched over Adam's shoulder, and it seemed as though Juliette was blissfully content and completely aware that she had just been carried to bed for the first time by her father.

With the baby tucked in, there was nothing more to do or say. As Adam walked back through the living room, he stepped on the pictures scattered on the floor. Evie felt a sudden, chilling premonition. Had he done it deliberately? she wondered. Could this be what the future holds for us? Whatever is unimportant to Adam will be stepped on. She felt a flash of ugly insight.

Suppose Adam didn't love either of them, but merely needed them to complete his personal vision of success? She knew a sickening dread that, whenever business opportunities called from that day on, he would treat Evie's feelings and Juliette's with the same contempt he'd just shown for the photographs he'd been faking such interest in earlier.

And if he trampled his child's heart, he would deny it, just as he'd done before with her. She avoided looking at him, and when they reached the door, he unbolted it himself without saying another word to her.

Maybe, she thought, maybe Adam is so driven by blind ambition that he doesn't realize what he's doing. After all, he's never known what it's like to be abandoned or resented. He's never spent a single unwanted day in his life. He never knew what it was like to have those who are supposed to love you the most desert you to the care of those who detest and resent you. He was always wanted, always loved, so he never knew the despair of being neither.

His footsteps echoed on the wooden stairs and he didn't touch the handrail or look down. Evie heard the metallic rattle of his keys and noticed that his spine and shoulders looked locked and rigid. She shivered and noticed that the night air had turned bitter.

Adam was halfway down the steps when Evie called to him, "You know what, Adam? Have you ever stopped to wonder why you've always taken love for granted?"

He turned to face her.

"It's because there was always plenty to go around in your family."

He was still looking up at her when she shut the door.

Olivia set a cup of tea down in front of Evie. "That sounds awful," she said. "Why didn't you wake me up."

Evie shook her head. "I don't know. I felt so drained. And besides, there really wasn't anything anyone could do. I made my bed," she said bitterly. "I guess I'll have to lie in it." Her words struck her as particularly ironic considering Adam's comment of the night before.

"How did the phone calls go?"

Evie sighed and rubbed her forehead. "If I ever hear one more shocked pause followed by the words, 'You're kidding,' I think I'll go insane."

"Bad?"

"Bad. Everybody blames me. Everybody acts like I'm the one who abandoned Adam. Nobody seems to remember he was gone for most of the last two years of our marriage, or that he was in South America the entire time I was pregnant." She shrugged a little sheepishly. "Although he didn't exactly *know* that I was expecting. The only person who didn't try to make me feel worse about everything was Aunt Nila, and that's because she doesn't care. She said she figured something like that was going on and that she never believed the Marlene story." Evie sighed. "My Aunt Nila is many things, but she's not dumb."

Olivia had a very I-told-you-so look on her face, but she was much too kind to say the words. Instead, she took a brisk and businesslike breath. "So tell me, what happens now?"

Evie sighed. "Well, I guess I pack up and move back to the house on Sunday." She gave her friend a wan smile. "There is a bright side. I can keep on working with you. That is—I mean, if you want me to."

"Don't be silly. Of course I want you to."

"It'll probably be part-time from now on."

"Anything suits me, as long as I can see you and my precious little angel."

Evie spent the rest of Thursday battling her growing feelings of frustration and humiliation. The more she thought of last night's conversation, the more she wished she'd handled things differently. She wished she'd have had the aplomb to stand up to him effectively and hit him with more articulate comebacks to his accusations.

But she'd felt guilty about being "caught," so she'd been defensive. Wimpy. She would have had a lot more to say if she hadn't been so scared. The more she thought of it, the madder she became. She had imaginary conversations with him in which she hit him with home truths that doubled him over. Why, she wondered furiously, do you always think of what you should have said when it's too late to say it?

She slammed drawers and carped so relentlessly at Eddie and Frank, the delivery drivers, they wouldn't stay in the same room with her. Olivia remained steadfastly cheerful and acted as if she didn't notice Evie's vile mood. She did, however, lunge for the phone every time it rang, obviously fearful that Evie would terrorize their clientele, and after lunch she tactfully sent Evie on an errand long enough to give her time to drive and think of a solution.

Unfortunately she couldn't think of a thing. For a moment, she toyed with the idea of proceeding with the divorce action, but she was positive Adam would make good on his threats to fight her for custody. The thought of him taking Juliette from her was chilling.

In her entire adult life, Evie had never been forced to do something she abhorred. The experience of being powerless maddened her to the point of frenzy. Part of her was still frightened of what Adam might do, but most of her wanted to punish him for making her feel this way. A niggling suggestion flitted through her mind that maybe, in some way, she had been trying to punish Adam for abandoning her by keeping Juliette from him. She scoffed. No way. She just wasn't that sort of person.

Later, after the shop closed, Olivia invited her for dinner, but she declined. She knew she'd be rotten company. The last thing she wanted to do was alienate her dearest, if not only, remaining friend. Instead she fed and bathed her daughter and began to pack up her kitchen for the movers.

At seven-thirty she was up to her elbows in boxes and newsprint when she heard a soft knocking at the door. She knew it wasn't Olivia. Livvie would have used the inside stairs or thumped their code on the wall they shared.

Evie narrowed her eyes. Suddenly she knew exactly who was knocking on her door. The nerve of him, she thought. She took her time rinsing her hands, then pulled the band out of her hair so it would stand up around her face like a lion's mane. She gave the silverware drawer a good slam, and then marched toward the front door to do battle with her husband.

When she yanked the door she gasped. A striking woman stood on the landing. She wore her thick, silver-streaked blond hair pulled into a chignon, and she looked impeccable, cool and shrewd in fine gray wool. Slung over her shoulder was a huge, obscenely expensive, Italian designer carryall, and in her hands she held, of all things, a plate of homemade cookies.

"Aunt Nila?" Evie said weakly. She felt as if she'd been punched.

Nila Delaney drew her brick red lips into a knowing smile. "Hello, darling. I thought you might need
a baby-sitter."

"And so I assumed if I phoned you to ask if I could
come see the baby, you'd tell me not to come because
it's such a horrible time. So I didn't call. I just came.
Richard's flying back from a conference in Hamburg
and I had to be in Houston, anyway. Lucky it was so
convenient for me."

Lucky it was so convenient for you?

Nila had been in the apartment for nearly half an
hour, and Evie still felt dumbfounded. The first thing
her aunt had done was insist on being shown Juliette.
She'd pronounced her "just darling," declined to hold
her and asked to be given a cup of tea. She sat on
Evie's divan with her long, elegant legs crossed at the
ankle and angled to one side to accommodate the tall
heels she wore.

"I'm just so amazed to see you," Evie said. "And
thank you for the gifts. The dresses are really pretty,
but most of all thanks for this." Evie reverently
touched an old, cloth-covered album. "I never even
knew my mother made a baby book for me. I can't tell
you what it means to have it. Having this makes me
feel like she's with me—like a guardian angel."

"Well," Nila said. "I've never been particularly
spiritual. I suppose that comes from living with a sci-
entist." She set her cup down on the table. "I nearly
threw it out with all your old clothes and toys, and at
the last minute I just stuck it in a drawer."

Evie swallowed. If she had known Nila had meant
to throw out her things, she would have gone to

Louisiana to get them. Or she could have called Mrs. Alexander, who would gladly have walked next door to collect them. If Nila had just phoned to ask...but, of course, she wouldn't think of it. Saying something about it was pointless; throwing her treasures away had not been malicious, just sadly typical.

"Well," Nila said, "I have to say I'm astounded at the courage you've shown. Of course, I always thought marrying Adam Rabalais was a mistake. I'm surprised your marriage lasted this long."

Evie felt suddenly cold. "I thought you liked Adam."

"Good heavens, I do. That's not what I meant. I believe Adam Rabalais is the finest young man who ever came through Evansville, Louisiana." She rolled her eyes. "Heavenly days, how did any of us end up there?" She looked back at her niece. "But you see, my dear, I've never seen two people more identical in temperament than the two of you. I believe that's called a very volatile mix."

Evie gave her aunt a skeptical look. "I'm sorry, but I disagree. We want completely different things."

"Of course you do," Nila said. "But it's your spirits—your essences—that are identical. When the two of you fell in love, I felt wistful. I thought I had a great love. But seeing you two together..." She looked away. "I've never seen anything like it. Despite the difference in your backgrounds, your interests and your families, I saw that there was a completely irresistible emotional force at work."

She looked back at Evie. "I knew that kind of intensity wouldn't burn out, but I felt certain it would explode."

Evie didn't answer right away. Was Nila right? She wondered. Had she been mistaken about Adam's actions? Could his compulsion about work be evidence of his love for her rather than his indifference? It didn't make sense.

"Well, tell me," Nila said. "What exactly was it that made you want out of your marriage?"

"To tell you the truth, I never wanted out of it. I just wanted my husband to show up at the house occasionally. I wanted to have children and some kind of family life, and now everything is ruined. He's going to be the same kind of father as Richard—" Evie blushed. "I'm sorry. I shouldn't have said that."

"It's all right," Nila said coolly. "Richard was an abominable stepparent and I wasn't any better. I'll never stop regretting the way I failed you, Evie, but I've had to go on. By the time you were ten or so I believe we all got the hang of it, but at first it was a nightmare for all of us. To put it bluntly, darling, you were just in the way. You know neither of us cared for children or planned to have any—"

"I know," Evie interrupted. She'd heard all this before. "But how can someone treat a child that way. He used to tell me that I ruined everything. That he couldn't stand the sight of me."

Nila patted her perfect hair. "You don't understand, Evangeline. There was a larger imperative at work. Richard is a great mind. His work has global repercussions, and that means sometimes sentimental considerations are secondary. He was unaccustomed to having children underfoot. He needed peace and quiet for his work."

Evie didn't argue with her. Some things are never mended or resolved. Some things just have to be accepted for what they are.

"Can I get you something else, Aunt Nila?"

"Darling," Nila said. "Do you think that dear Mrs. Delcomb would watch the darling baby and let us go out to dinner? I feel I'd like something horribly sinful. You know, I haven't had decent Mexican food in years."

"I'd love to, Aunt Nila, but I have to pack."

"All right then."

Nila stood, gathered her things and kissed the air next to Evie's cheek. She didn't ask to see Juliette again.

Chapter Eight

A squad of movers invaded Evie's flat at ten o'clock Sunday morning and accomplished the packing and loading of her things with the precision of a military exercise. By eleven-thirty the entire contents of her home were padded, stowed and tied down in a ridiculously oversize office equipment van. Evie waved *au revoir* to Olivia and led the way. At exactly ten minutes before twelve, she pulled into the driveway of the house she never thought she'd see again. Much less occupy.

The bungalow sat on a shaded lot on a quiet cul-de-sac in an older section of West University Place. Many of the houses like this one, modest homes built in the fifties, had since been bought as tear-downs so the wealthy and up-and-coming could erect imposing new edifices on the deep, quiet and beautifully shaded lots close to Rice University.

On Adam and Evie's street, though, most of the houses had merely been updated. An architect friend of Adam's had worked with Evie to enhance the cozy feel of the house while opening it up to allow light to pour in.

Part of her was thrilled to be seeing the house again, while another part of her felt only dread. She sighed as some of her fears were realized; the azaleas were reedy with neglect, and the wisteria, left completely without discipline, was crawling all over the roof. The ligustrums were a misshapen mess and the pyracantha was spiky and lethal looking with unpruned, foot-long shoots just waiting to snare an unwary pant leg or sweater.

Evie looked down at her passenger-side occupant, snugly strapped into her padded car seat. "It looks like we've got our work cut out for us, wouldn't you say?"

Juliette, intent on the further study of her toes, attempted no reply. Evie sighed. She certainly wasn't going to be wiling away endless hours in the backyard like she used to. She smiled. Now she had something much better to do.

In moments the van rolled into the driveway behind her, and she stepped out of her car. Years ago, when Adam first bought it without consulting her, she hadn't particularly liked the sedan. She'd thought it much too staid and boxy for her tastes, but Adam had insisted she have it because the make had a reputation for being practically indestructible. Later on she'd become thankful to have it.

While the men let down the ramp, Evie fumbled with her key ring. A messenger from Adam's office had arrived at the shop Friday afternoon with a new set of keys and the garage door opener she'd left on the table the last time she was in the house. Adam hadn't enclosed a note, and Evie had seethed for hours after receiving the package. It struck as a silent order. *Get to the house or else!*

Now, though, she couldn't help but feel a hint of excitement about returning. She had loved this house and its garden. She might have been happy here.

Evie knew the unloading wouldn't take long because she had so little furniture. She'd rented the apartment from Olivia almost completely furnished. The crib and baby furniture she'd been using were family pieces Olivia had insisted she use while she stayed there, but of course she couldn't bring them with her when she left. The only large pieces she'd taken with her when she'd fled this house nearly a year ago were the antiques she'd inherited from her mother.

For fifteen years, Richard and Nila had stored them for her in their unused guest house. Evie had finally taken them when she and Adam had bought their first home. She loved the frail, old pieces and made elaborate, dire and only partly facetious threats to the movers about scratches and chipped feet.

There was the Civil War bed in which her great-great-grandfather had been born—and died—along with its matching wardrobe. These had always been in the guest room because the bed was too short for Adam and he refused to sleep in it. The armoire, of course, didn't go with anything else they had. Next came the Black Forest chair, then the secretary. All plodded back into the house on the sturdy shoulders of Adam's movers and were returned to the still-empty places they'd formerly occupied in the front bedroom.

Evie directed the placement of the furniture because Adam wasn't home. She wasn't really surprised. She hadn't expected him to be anywhere else but at work. *Start the way you mean to go on.*

Most of the kitchen things were sent straight to the attic; the books and small decorative items were left behind the wet bar in the den, and she instructed that the boxes and cartons of her clothing be left in the living room. She intended to sort all that out later. She set her jaw. If Adam wanted to keep the atmosphere in their home chilly, she would comply. Enthusiastically.

When all was accomplished, Evie thanked the men and tipped the driver enough to share with his helpers. The next task, she knew, would be more arduous—deciding where to put her clothes. Instead of facing that immediately, she fed Juliette and waited until the baby fell asleep. Then she slowly reacquainted herself with her home.

The kitchen seemed the same except for the conspicuous absence of her magnificent airplane plant. Probably expired from neglect, she thought. Her fault, really. Dining room unchanged. Ditto for the hall bath. She padded quietly through, touching and remembering.

She wondered where Adam would make room for the nursery. There were four bedrooms, she'd already seen the front guest room, and the next one had been his study. She couldn't imagine him giving it up. She pushed the door open. Sure enough, nothing had changed. His desk, file cabinets and bookcases were all as they had been. A Rand-McNally map of the world covered one wall and bristled with colored push pins showing the places Adam had been.

French doors looked out over the multilevel deck and across the yard to the mimosas and the tattered calla lilies and hibiscus. Actually, she thought, she wouldn't have liked this room for the nursery, anyway. Too far away from the master bedroom. And, besides, the French doors leading directly into the baby's room would make her nervous.

She'd assumed that Adam would dictate where Juliette's things would go by clearing a place for her. This, Evie thought, would also tell her whether he was serious when he said he didn't care to share their room with her. Since he'd kept his office intact, and hadn't changed the antique bedroom, she assumed he'd cleared a space for the baby, and perhaps for her as well, in the room they called the bachelor bedroom—named for the simple furnishings from Adam's college days.

Maybe he'd have cleared it all out now, and she would open the door to see a narrow single bed pushed against the far wall and covered with only an itchy army blanket. *That'll be just fine with me. If he wants it that way....*

Don't be stupid. He wouldn't do that.

Would he?

She pushed the door open and stood riveted to the spot. The room was freshly and cheerfully painted in a pink so pale it was only a wash of color. The baseboards and crown moldings gleamed with brilliant white enamel and extravagantly thick sheers covered the windows, but a second rod had been set and appeared to be waiting for someone to quit dallying around and hang the curtains.

The only piece of furniture in the room was a child-size rocking chair, occupied by a small, wistful-looking teddy bear. Evie saw a card tied around the bear's wrist, and when she picked him up she read, "To Juliette, with all my love, Daddy."

Daddy.

The name struck her as unbearably poignant, and she choked up immediately.

Juliette was going to have a daddy. Evie barely remembered her own father, and knew him only as a thin, fair-skinned young man smiling sheepishly at her from one of the rare photographs of him she had. His hair was a blue-black tangle of ringlets and he wore hideous bell-bottom blue jeans. She remembered that he played "Catch A Falling Star" on the mandolin and that he made her mother laugh. That was all.

The child who still lived somewhere inside her had never forgiven him for leaving her. She took a tremulous breath. Maybe that contributed to her anger at Adam. Maybe, just maybe, she was punishing him for the unintentional sins of others. She brushed her tears away.

But things were going to be different for Juliette. At least she hoped so. The teddy bear made her think Adam meant to try.

She stopped to think for a moment. If she and Adam established an atmosphere of armed truce in their home, who would suffer? Not just the two of them but Juliette, as well. Evie had read enough to know that small children are aware of tension and hostility, even when they don't understand it. She didn't want that for her child.

She didn't want that for herself.

This was where she was going to live for an undetermined amount of time. This is where her child would be raised. She would have to make the best of it—and not reluctantly, either, because both Adam and Juliette would sense that. She would try, as best she could, to go onward from here positively and constructively. Maybe this situation wasn't the best, but she had a choice to make it either worse or better.

She knew then what she needed to do.

Just as she leaned over to put the toy back in the chair, she noticed an envelope on the floor behind the rocker. It had been addressed to her in Adam's strong, slanted hand. Inside was a platinum charge card and a folded note.

"Olivia told me the baby needed furniture. Please get whatever you think is best. Adam."

She read it twice and sighed. She looked into the bear's round, button eyes. "Not exactly a cuddly message, is it, Ted?" She dropped the bear back in the chair and checked the closet. Empty. That didn't necessarily mean anything. After all, what would he hang in the closet to indicate he expected her to put her clothes there?

Well, one more room to go, she thought, and headed down the hall. Nostalgia hit her in a wave. Nothing was different. Not just the furniture and pictures in the room, but the atmosphere and smells appeared to have been undisturbed by her absence. Even the uninteresting book she'd been reading the night before she left was still waiting on her nightstand where she'd left it months ago. Adam's housekeeper obviously dusted it faithfully every week, and then put it right back where it was.

Other things also remained unchanged. Adam's running shorts lay in a silver pool where he'd stepped out of them earlier that day, and although one shoe sat upright, the other appeared to have fallen over from exhaustion. Evie knew she'd find his socks on the way to the bathroom. *Slob,* she thought, with quiet amusement. If Adam hadn't taken his daily run shirtless, she knew she'd find that lying in a sweaty pile somewhere close to the front door.

There was one thing left to do. She crossed the room and took a deep, calming breath and opened their closet door. Her rod was empty and waiting. She felt a glimmer of hope. Maybe this meant he also intended to try to make this reconciliation work. Maybe he wanted to help repair the damage they'd done.

Or maybe, since he was always gone, he just hadn't bothered to rearrange his clothes.

Leaving the door open, Evie turned to gather up his clothes and throw them in the laundry basket. She got on her knees to look under the bed for the missing socks, and that's when she saw the plastic bag. She frowned. The bag was from Spoon and Lockwood, a criminally overpriced bookstore in The Village. She pulled the bag out and sat on the floor.

The titles made her heart ache. *It's a Girl! (Now What?). How To Be the Best Dad in the World. Your Baby, the First Year.* The last one had obviously been read the most. Pages had been dog-eared, a maddening habit of Adam's, and the first several chapters had notes scrawled in their margins, and whole passages had been highlighted in yellow.

Evie bit her trembling lower lip. These were the pages dealing with delivery, bringing the baby home and the first few months of life. Adam had apparently been trying to experience those things in the pages of a book, since she'd taken them from him.

The thought of him sitting alone in the house, reading his book and trying to capture some of the most beautiful moments Evie had ever known filled her with grief for him. She tried to imagine what she would feel like if someone had kept Juliette from her for the first three months of her precious life. She squeezed her eyes shut. The pain would be unendurable. Would he ever be able to forgive her for hurting him this way, robbing him of those times?

I'm sorry. I thought you didn't want us.

She leaned against the bed, buried her face in the crook of her elbow and tried to hold back her tears. Those moments are gone forever, she thought. Photographs in a book weren't even a pale shadow of those experiences. Gone. All gone.

The weight of her guilt clamped around her chest, and she wondered if she'd ever get over the suffocating feeling. Adam's words came back to her. *What have you done?*

Then something else occurred to her. She had done the best she could with the information she'd had at the time. Maybe she had made mistakes, but she wasn't the only one. Adam had not been there for her in times when she'd needed him desperately. Maybe he hadn't meant them, but he had said harsh words, almost cruel words.

They had both played parts in this damaged marriage. She sniffled a loud and undignified sniffle.

And it was up to both of them to fix it. Far away she heard an unmistakable cry and knew Juliette was feeling insecure, left alone in unfamiliar surroundings. Evie stood and ran lightly down the hall to the kitchen.

The baby blinked and whacked the air in outrage. Evie discovered she was damp and grabbed her diaper bag. Then she picked up her daughter and took her to the bedroom to change her on the enormous king-size bed.

Hours later, Evie was awakened by a sudden weight settling on the bed beside her. She looked up into rain-colored eyes and sighed.

"Hello," she said.

"Hello."

"I fell asleep."

"Both of you did."

The sun was slanting through the curtains, and Evie knew it was close to sunset. "I hope you don't mind me sleeping here."

"This is your bed, too, Evie. Where else should you sleep?"

His voice and face were reaching out to her, but she could see that he was still wary. Still hurt. She was, too.

"I've been thinking," he said.

"Me, too," she said, and pulled herself into a sitting position.

"There's probably a lot we need to talk about."

"I know."

"But first, can't we just try to make this work?"

"I want to."

He looked over at Juliette, sleeping in her carrier. "Not just for—I mean, not just because of Juliette."

She nodded. Now was the time to reach out. To try to start a healing. "I couldn't stand living without you. I never wanted to. But when—"

He held up a hand to stop her. "Not yet," he said. "First there's something I want to give you. It's important to me."

He wore his ancient denim jacket, and he reached into the pocket and pulled out a small velvet pouch. He didn't hand it to her, but opened it himself and took out a wide gold band, aglitter with baguettes. Evie swallowed. Shards of splintered light danced from the ring. *He wants this to work, too. We have a chance.*

"It's incredible," she said. "So different from...the other one."

"I know," he said, and took her left hand. "I thought it needed to be."

Next to them Juliette made a dove sound, and Evie turned and saw the baby regarding her parents with a serious, interested expression. Evie looked back at Adam and saw the beginnings of a smile soften his mouth and nearly reach his eyes.

He slipped the ring on her finger, and the unaccustomed feel of it was heavy and pleasant. The ring, of course, was staggering. She looked at her husband, leaned forward and kissed him on the mouth.

He held her lightly in his arms and stroked her hair and pressed her gently against his body. He sighed. At that moment she wanted nothing more than to be held in his welcoming and healing embrace. Other healings would come later in their own time, but for now, the first step was forgiveness.

And in their family they had plenty to go around.

Almost an hour later Evie was still propped on her side watching the baby, and Adam lay behind her, his knees curved into hers and his chin resting lightly on her shoulder. He called this "spooning." They'd always gone to sleep in the spoon position though they sometimes tossed away from each other during the night. Juliette had been entertaining them with her bird calls and vowel sounds for the past half hour, and motes now danced in the shafts of fading sunlight that streaked through the bedroom window.

Although Adam had held Evie in his arms for a long time, some tacit, unspoken agreement stopped any further intimacy. They were now moving slowly and carefully with each other, their words and movements tentative—like two people trying to learn the steps of an elaborate and complicated new dance.

At that moment, though, Evie was in paradise, lying between the two people she loved most in the world and doing something she loved—sharing Juliette wholeheartedly with her father for the first time. They stared at her as if she were some fascinating and exotic art exhibit.

Adam moved his hand to Evie's hip and his thumb began a slow, deep massage of her lower back. She moaned an acknowledgement and turned her head fractionally to press her cheek to his.

He sighed. "Sweetheart?"

"Mmm?"

"What did you look like when you were pregnant?"

She paused and let her breath out in a huff. "I don't know. Illinois? Wyoming? Pick any of the middle-size states."

He chuckled. "You got big?"

"Huge. I couldn't move. I couldn't sleep. I slept in the shop for the last month because I couldn't go up the stairs." She turned over onto her back and touched his cheek. "I have some pictures. I'll show them to you, but then you have to forget you ever saw me look like that."

He backed away from her and screwed his face into a squint. First he tipped his head to one side, then the other.

"What are you doing?"

He didn't answer. Instead he pulled one of the pillows from the top of the bed and laid it on her stomach.

She started to laugh.

"Were you this big?"

"I wish. You'll have to get all of them and then go borrow a few from the neighbors." She rolled her eyes. "They used a forklift to get me on the gurney."

His laughter faded a little. "But you're . . . I mean, you got—"

"I know." She shrugged. "It all fell off. And then I got thinner than before." She looked sadly at her chest. "There wasn't much to start with, was there? And now look at me."

The amusement returned to his eyes. "Okay. I think I should." She was wearing a soft black turtleneck and he grabbed the hem and began to pull it up.

Evie laughed and grabbed his wrist, "Please! Not in front of the children."

Juliette chose that moment to let out a piercing, tin-whistle squeal. Adam and Evie both gasped and looked at the baby who looked as startled as they were at the shrillness and volume of the noise she could make.

"She's going to be an opera star," Adam said. "Or a champion hog caller."

"Honey," Evie said. "You ain't heard nothing yet. She can do that for hours."

Adam's gaze snapped back to hers. "You're kidding."

She shook her head. "Hours," she repeated.

The baby reddened and began to struggle like an overturned tortoise. Evie reached over to her. "Wet again," she said. "Have you been out drinking with your friends while my back was turned?" She popped a quick kiss on Adam's cheek. "'Scuse me, honey. Duty calls."

"I'll do it," he said, and in an instant he had crossed the room and was searching through Evie's diaper bag. He took out the wipes and powder and had the baby freshly diapered in only moments. Evie, dumbfounded, watched in silence.

"Something tells me that's not the first time you've done that."

"It isn't." He held the baby over his shoulder and Evie noticed that his palm was wide enough to completely cover her back. "You forget, I'm the oldest of four. I had to help out with the younger kids." He looked back at his daughter. "And I've also taken some instructions lately."

"When? Who from?"

"Olivia."

"What?"

"Yeah," he said, bouncing in place and pressing Juliette's hand to his lips. "Last Thursday."

"Thursday? But . . . where was I?"

"On the bogus errand Olivia thought up to get you out of everybody's way."

Evie frowned. "She didn't tell me."

"She's going to. I just asked her not to until you had moved back here." His delighted expression grew solemn. "Don't be angry with her, Evie. She didn't know

I was coming, and she only agreed about waiting to tell you under duress.''

"So," Evie asked. "Did you come to see me when I wasn't there?"

He looked her straight in the eyes. "No. I called the shop because I wanted to see Juliette. The fact that you weren't there just turned out to be a convenient circumstance. I wasn't ready to talk to you, and I didn't figure you had much to say to me, either. But I just had to see my baby."

Evie swallowed. She had to admit she understood that. "So, on Thursday." She grew thoughtful. "Was that the only time?"

"No. Friday, too. You were gone to the—"

"Grocery store."

"Right," he said. "I would have come on Saturday, but you stayed home all day packing."

"I see." She looked up at him. "We're going to have to learn to communicate better, you know?"

He nodded. "Funny, isn't it? We talked all the time, but some important stuff didn't get said. Or didn't get heard."

Evie sighed and sat up. "Where do we start?"

"I'm not sure." He shrugged. "I feel like we're doing okay now."

Yes, Evie thought, but so far nothing has come up that could cause any conflict.

Evie suddenly laughed. "Did Olivia tell you who showed up on Thursday?"

Adam grinned. "Aunt Marble Heart."

Evie scowled at him. "Oh, well, try to be nice. She's just about all the family I've got left. Things won't ever be exactly warm and cuddly between us, but I think I can be generous."

"I'd like to see her again," Adam said. He rolled his eyes. "I never thought I'd hear myself say that."

Evie smiled. "Me, either."

"How's Uncle . . . Richard?"

"Same. Brilliant. Cuckoo as ever. Just back from some terribly significant conference."

"He used to scare me. I'd be trying like hell to make conversation with him, and in the middle of a sentence he'd suddenly jump up, run out of the room, down the hall and slam the door."

Evie chuckled. "You should be flattered. You know that means something you said gave him some kind of idea."

Their gazes crossed, touched and then held for a moment. These small. things, sharing memories, laughing together again—these were the substance of healing and of rebuilding bridges. Evie looked down at her hand on the bedspread and admired her ring. "I'd like to go back to Evansville." She glanced up quickly. "For a visit, I mean."

Adam smiled gently. "I know that's what you meant."

She sat up. "I have wonderful memories from there. That place, that poky little town is where my dreams came true."

Adam's face grew tender. "Oh, sweetheart," he murmured.

Evie took a deep breath. "I know I've never told you this, but as soon as I met you, I thought that something magical had happened, like in a book. My life—well, all of it that I could remember—had been so... mean and lonely. When you walked in, I knew right away that you were the one who would give the story of my life a happy ending."

"You know," he said quietly. "There... there are a lot of things—stories that I've never told you. Things I wanted to put behind me and out of my life because I wanted to have a different, well, like you said, life story. I wanted to be good enough."

"Good enough? For what? That's ridiculous." Although Evie knew what Adam was talking about, she felt compelled to launch into a litany of his accomplishments—just as she had done before. "You were the most popular boy in school. One of the smartest. You were captain of the baseball team, class president—"

"Evie," he said, stopping her with a look. "Do you remember the first time you saw my family?"

Her gaze fell. "Yes," she said quietly. She'd never forget the first time she'd seen Curtis, Naomi and the other three Rabalais children piling into the smoke-belching, primer-tinted pickup Curtis drove. They reminded Evie of the Joad family from *The Grapes of Wrath*. They drove away, leaving Adam with the Alexanders because he wanted to go to Evansville High for his senior year.

"Don't get me wrong. I love and respect my parents and how hard they worked, but chasing the oil rigs all over the South was not exactly a glamorous life-style."

"I know it was hard."

But Evie wondered how much she did know. Adam had never talked much about the past. With him it was always plans for the future.

"Someday," he said. "I'm going to have to tell you some stories that I tried to forget. Maybe there's some answers for us in some of that."

Evie nodded. "I think so."

Juliette had fallen back asleep, and Adam carefully laid her in her little carrier. Evie slid down to the end of the bed and curled herself against Adam's body, and he leaned over and took her back into the shelter of his arms.

She buried her face against him for a moment and then curved her head back to look up at his face. "Kiss," she said, and he did, sweetly and tenderly, but with the promise of other less-restrained moments to come.

"How long will she sleep?" Adam asked.

Evie shrugged and wrapped her arms tighter around his waist. "Don't know. But I've got an idea," she said with a sly look. "That is, if you want to make me *very* happy."

The deep chuckle in Adam's chest moved through her like the rumble of bass notes in loud music. "Oh, yeah." His hands slid over her shoulders and down her back and she arched herself against him.

The amused look in his eyes began a deep transformation. "What's that?" he asked.

She grinned. "Take us shopping."

Chapter Nine

"What do you think of these?" Evie asked thoughtfully. "I really love the sun theme, don't you?"

Adam scowled. "Too much yellow." He looked at Juliette, who rode in the crook of his arm. "Nope, she doesn't like 'em, either. Ugly old yellow."

Evie gave him an exasperated look. "Well, what color is the sun supposed to be? Chartreuse?"

Adam shrugged. "I don't know. I don't care. But these don't exactly adhere to the concept of ruthless, photographic realism, do they? Since when does the sun have eyebrows?"

Evie made a growly noise in her throat. "What am I going to do with you? Just what exactly have you got against yellow? It's so happy."

And so, standing there in the middle of the baby-outlet mall, he told her the story of the nightmares, the screaming locomotive and the woman in the Easter-egg yellow dress who told him he was trailer trash.

Stunned into silence, Evie could only stare up at him, blinking back tears of pain and hurt for the little boy he had been and for the innocence destroyed in that moment of cruelty. "That's so sad," she said. "Why didn't you ever tell me before?"

Adam studied her. "I suppose it's because that's one of the things in my past I most wanted to distance myself from. If I'd told you, it would have been the same as dragging it along with me."

"But don't you think you have? I mean, the way you hate—dislike—the color that reminds you of that incident." Evie pressed her lips together and she narrowed her eyes. "I'd love to run into that woman."

Adam smiled. "Me, too...in a half-ton pickup."

They both laughed and she leaned into him, giving a little comfort and taking a little in simple affection.

"I suppose," he said, "in a way it turned out to be a good experience. After that I decided to work as hard and as long as I had to—to do anything necessary to prove what she called me wasn't true."

Evie looked straight into his eyes. "But, sweetheart, that's called *being driven*." Her tone was serious, but she'd conscientiously tried to keep it from sounding accusatory.

"So? What's wrong with that?"

"Well, it's hard to say, but wouldn't it be better if your motivation was in front of you rather than behind you? To be inspired? If you're inspired you can attain a goal, but if you're driven, how do you know when you've gotten far enough away?''

He looked down at her for a moment, and she thought she saw something fearful skip through his eyes. But then he just shrugged and looked away. Then he looked back at her and grinned, obviously wanting to lighten the mood. "Maybe you stop having nightmares." He walked away from Evie, holding Juliette up high in the air and making funny faces and motorboat noises at her.

"Adam," Evie said in exasperation, "come back. Wait for me. What nightmares? What's that supposed to mean?''

He was far ahead of her, though, head thrown back, laughing at his daughter. "I know I can make her laugh," he said. "I don't care what your doctor says. She's a prodigy. After all, look at her father." He looked over his shoulder at Evie. "Get whatever sheets and stuff you want. We're going over here to sporting goods. I think my baby needs a good bat—a Louisville Slugger. And a really good glove. I think she'll play shortstop. On the boys' team."

He walked away holding her high in his arms. "Come on, Julie-Beans, let's go show off to the other babies. You can be nice even though you're so-o-o much prettier than they are." Though his laugh was quiet and deep, the rumble of it carried back to where Evie stood. "But you can't be nice to the boy babies," he said. "Wait till you're thirty. Or forty. Daddy will come on your dates with you. Won't that be fun?''

Evie planted her hands on her hips, scowled and tried to look threatening. Since he never looked back the gesture was wasted, and she had to content herself by muttering an unflattering anatomical reference at his retreating back. Then she went to find the sales clerk in the linen section. "We've decided on the...the jungle sheets." She said.

Many hundreds of dollars later, the three of them were headed back toward town on the Southwest Freeway. The only large item they packed into Adam's car was a magnificent cherry wood crib in a Victorian sleigh bed style, so Juliette would have her own bed to sleep in that night. The bed was outrageously over-priced, and Evie thought it was preposterous to spend that amount of money on furniture she'd outgrow in just a few years, but Adam insisted. The other furniture items were to be delivered the next day.

Juliette, oblivious of the small fortune being spent on her, had slept through most of the process.

"Hungry?" Adam asked.

"Always," Evie said.

"Mexican?"

"*¡Cómo no!*" She gave him a mischievous smile. "That's Spanish for 'Yes, why not.'"

"Evangeline," Adam said drolly, "I speak four languages."

"Show-off," she said, and dusted his arm with a light punch. She faced forward with anticipation. "I could eat Mexican food every day," she said.

"And you'd be as *grande* as *una vaca,* too." He looked over at her with a sly smile, "That's Spanish for big as a cow."

"So what? It'd be worth it. Besides, you'd still want me."

He glanced over at her. "Yes," he said, "I would."

"La Jaliscience?"

"You don't want to go somewhere fancy? I mean, we're dressed."

"Nope, La Jali is my fave."

"Okay. To La Jali."

Twenty minutes later they sat in the old *taqueria* next to the Laundromat on the corner of Montrose and West Gray. A small bowl of pickled vegetables, mouth-blistering with jalapeños and serrano peppers, sat on the table between them along with tortilla chips, salsa, *queso* and two frosty beers with wedges of lime languishing at the bottom of the mugs. Cheese enchiladas, *pollo asado* and sides of rice and beans were on their way.

The fifty-year-old restaurant squatted at the crossroads of River Oaks—which meant old money and lots of it—and the bohemian community of Montrose with its art bars, alternative music and coffeehouses. The building itself was ancient, the ceiling sagging and water spotted. When it rained heavily, buckets and bus tubs had to be strategically placed around the dining area, and some of the tables were rendered unusable because of the steady trickle of water from overhead.

"I love this old place," Adam said.

"Me, too."

Although the restaurant was crowded with Sunday evening diners, they were still able to take their favorite booth. Adam liked it because he could see who was coming in the front door. Evie liked it because she had an unimpeded view of her favorite element in the restaurant besides the magnificent but inexpensive food. She gazed up and smiled at it, still fascinated after years.

The stuffed black head of a bull stared solemnly down from atop the arched doorway leading into the other dining room. The brown marbles in his eye sockets were cloudy and eccentrically positioned, and the head hung slightly tilted on the wall while a graceful beard of dust trailed from his long, coarse chin hairs. The animal had obviously died in a *corrida* because his ears had been ceremonially taken.

The taxidermist—Evie assumed in a fit of artistic whimsy—had painted his nose gunmetal gray and had overstuffed the animal's cheeks until they puffed out. He had, she thought, the wistful, resigned look of a dinner guest who had something unpleasant in his mouth, but was much too polite to spit it out.

Evie took a sip of her beer. "Can I ask you something?"

"'Course."

"What happened after that day? The day you were supposed to go to the country club? Did you ever see Beth again?"

Adam sighed. "No. We moved again. I told you, I went to nearly twenty schools before we got to Evansville. The next placed we lived was close to Midland. My first experience with Texas dust storms. We stayed there until I was eleven. Good things happened there— the best teacher I ever had, my dad started doing welding so there was more money. And I learned the most valuable lesson of my life.''

''Yeah?''

Adam finished the last of his beer in one long drink and signaled the waiter to bring him another. ''You ready?'' he asked.

She lifted her hands. ''No, thanks. I'd like some tea, though.'' Evie sat on her side of the booth, wallowing in the luxury of eating an entire meal without interruption. Adam insisted that he be the one to take care of the baby while Evie enjoyed their first dinner.

Adam dug an enormous chip out of the basket, loaded it with cheese, salsa and then piled it high with peppers and pickled onions. Evie gave a little cringe. ''Ow, that's a hot one.''

''You know me.''

She smiled, but she wondered, do I? ''So what was this valuable lesson?''

Adam wiped his hands and washed his blazing mouth with the cold beer the waiter placed in front of him. ''Well, on my thirteenth birthday, my dad brought home a basketball. But not just any basketball. It was brand new. One of the only new gifts I ever had. The ball was signed by that year's NBA All-Stars. My dad told me the head tool pusher won it in a poker game in Odessa, and he got it from him because . . .''

On that day Adam had been giddy with euphoria. He'd never had such a ball—much less owned one. He wanted to race through the cake-and-ice-cream part of his party so he could go shoot hoops at the junior high basketball court. On Saturday afternoon there were always other kids there, and he wanted to show off his treasure.

Earl had to be brought along, but Adam didn't really mind. His younger brother would sit on the sidelines and watch and not try to play with the older guys. Adam even let him carry the basketball. Earl marched along as proudly as a standard bearer.

As soon as they turned the corner and were in plain sight of the court, Adam's heart lurched. Poochie Damrell and two of his cronies were already playing triples with a ball Adam knew they'd stolen from the school.

Poochie had been held back twice, so although he was in Adam's class, he was fifteen. He was a mean boy, toughened by the beatings that his mother passed along from his father. Everyone in the Damrell family always appeared to have just fallen off a bicycle— covered in bruises and scrapes in various stages of healing.

Adam knew it would be wisest to turn and run, but that would have been unworthy of the basketball. He couldn't keep himself from freezing momentarily in fright, though. Poochie had a kind of radar for that sort of thing and hooted with glee as soon as he saw them.

"Lookie here," he said. "It's Madam."

Poochie always corrupted names into something sexual or derogatory. Adam felt a wave of nausea, but stood his ground. There was absolutely no doubt about what was going to happen next, or anything that he could do about it. Adam again considered trying to flee, but he knew even if he could outrun them, Earl couldn't.

He took the ball from Earl who stood silently, eyes enormous, at his right elbow.

"Whatcha got there, Madam?"

"What's it look like?"

Poochie's face grew hard, then an evil smile twisted his round face. "I need me a new basketball. Here. Trade."

"No."

Poochie advanced on him, eyeing the ball Adam clutched to his middle. Older, thirty pounds heavier, and unburdened by integrity, morals or a modicum of fairness, Poochie walked up smiling and without hesitation punched Adam hard in the face. Adam fell like a tree and the ball rolled away. Then Poochie, for good measure, shoved Earl down.

"Thanks, Madam," he said, and looked up grinning at his companions.

Adam launched himself up like a ground-to-air missile and struck Poochie between his shoulders. Although he hit the bully from behind, at the time this tactic couldn't be considered a chicken move because Poochie had already turned around and was walking away to finish stealing Adam's ball. Besides, Poochie hardly noticed the stringy boy whacking ineffectively at his shoulders.

He merely paused in his stride, then turned around and calmly broke Adam's nose.

Adam was crying, streaming blood and using his limited vocabulary of curses, but he refused to give up his ball. Abandoning his treasure to a petty, vicious toad like Poochie Damrell would be cowardice beyond redemption. So he fought. In his own way.

Earl was screaming, the other boys were laughing and pointing, but they, too, eventually grew uneasy and nauseated at the beating Poochie was administering. Adam, however, refused to surrender. Every time Poochie flattened him, he got back up and flung himself, still crying back on the boy's fat shoulders.

The fight was finally over when Poochie was crying in angry frustration, out of breath, and too exhausted to continue knocking Adam down. Adam kept his ball, and the doctor at the Emergency Room, who was an understanding man, let him hold it while he stitched him up.

From that day on Poochie called him Adam.

"And I suppose that's when I learned not to ever give up," he said. "Just hang on, stick to your guns no matter what, and you'll succeed."

Evie didn't know whether to laugh or cry. "I thought I knew you inside out," she said. "There are so many things that I—that you never told me."

He shrugged. "You know the important stuff."

Through the rest of the dinner Evie wondered if she did.

Juliette had passed out in her carrier and slept through the meal and although Evie was grateful for the respite, she hoped this didn't mean the little girl was going to be awake all night long.

They were home by nine, and Juliette's bed was assembled and made up with jungle-theme sheets by ten-thirty. While Adam rocked her to sleep and put her down, Evie showered. She had just finished blowing her hair dry when Adam went in to take his shower.

Evie sat on the edge of her bed wrapped in her robe. A knot of anxiety had formed in her stomach, and she didn't know what to do. She'd been married for more than eight years; she'd known her husband since she was fourteen years old; but at that moment she felt overwhelmed with shyness and a completely uncharacteristic reluctance.

Evie had drawers full of negligees, silk pajamas and peignoir sets. She owned baby-dolls and teddies and some outrageous scraps of lace and elastic more suitable for a couch dancer than an upscale, suburban wife and mother.

But she wasn't quite sure what she wanted to say here.

Come hither?

Not really.

Peek-a-boo?

Hell, no.

Hi, there, sailor. Buy me a drink?

Not in this lifetime.

She loved Adam, she wanted to make her marriage work, but the truth was she just wasn't ready yet. The intimacy, surrender and all the tender indignities of lovemaking required a trust and willingness to be vulnerable she hadn't yet recaptured. But if she refused to be intimate with him, the fragile new beginning they were attempting would be damaged.

But then again, if she made love with him despite the way she felt, Adam would know. And then he'd be hurt. Bedroom relationships could have powerful re-

percussions in a marriage. What if he thought that she
didn't want to make love anymore because of the
baby. She heard that women often loose interest after
childbirth.

What if Adam blamed Juliette for ruining their sex
life? What if—what if—? Her mind raced on through
a variety of elaborate, unpleasant scenarios. She took
a calming breath. This is ridiculous, she thought. Get
a grip. She saw that her hands were shaking.

Then the water in the shower turned off. She heard
the slide of the shower door, followed soon after by the
hum of Adam's blow dryer. Evie fidgeted, riffled furiously through the things she'd hastily unpacked and
shoved into her lingerie drawers. This? No. This? Oh,
my God.

In the end she put on what she'd always worn to bed
before—a pair of panties and one of Adam's oversize
T-shirts. Then she yanked the shams off the bed, flung
back the comforter and dived into the sheets. She sat
there for a moment, back stiff and hands folded on her
lap.

Oh, my God, I look like I'm praying.

She switched on her light and opened the nightstand drawer to look for something to read. The mag-
azines were nearly a year old, as were the novelty
condoms lying beneath them. She slammed the drawer
on her finger and cursed.

The blow dryer shut off and Adam called, "You all
right?"

"Fine," she called.

She heard water running in the sink and the unmistakable noises of tooth brushing and mouthwash. A

drawer slid open and in a few moments shut quietly. She thought of the contents she'd just seen in the nightstand drawer and felt herself blanching.

Then the bathroom door opened and Adam walked out in a cloud of steam.

She smiled in spite of herself. He was tanned from working and running outside without his shirt. His upper body was only lightly dusted with hair, and his chest and stomach were rock solid from hard work and good genes. He'd never been a particularly muscular man, and age had smoothed his sharp angles, but he still had the best legs she'd ever seen. He'd kept his athlete's arms, too.

He wore for bed, as he always had before, boxer shorts.

For a moment he stood in the doorway, and then, with a slight smile, he crossed his arms and leaned against the jamb. "You look as nervous as I feel," he said.

Evie's breath rushed out. She didn't realize she'd been holding it. "Oh, Adam, I feel like a kid. I'm scared out of my mind."

Chuckling, he walked forward and sat down on his side of the bed. "Me, too."

Their laughter, again, brought them closer. "If you want me to," he said tentatively, "I could sleep in the other room."

"No!"

He blinked in surprise. "It wouldn't mean—"

"I know." She sighed. "I know we can't just pretend that nothing has ever gone wrong between us. I want things to be like . . . but we can't just . . . just—"

"No," he said. "We can't. But I didn't want you to feel that I didn't want to—" he encompassed what was left unsaid with a motion of his hand "—that I didn't want this. I thought that maybe since the baby came, you'd think that I didn't think you were still as sexy as all-get-out, when I do."

"You do?"

"I always have."

She sighed. "Then what do we do now?"

He tilted his head to the side and raked his hair.

"We could just spoon and go to sleep."

"Oh, sweetheart, that's exactly what I want to do."

They each turned off their lights and met in the middle of the bed. Evie turned on her side and faced the window, and Adam curled himself around her. His warm legs tucked into the bend of her knees, and he gathered her to him with one arm while he pillowed her head with the other. Then he smoothed her hair away from her neck and kissed her behind her ear. She giggled and curled up tighter. "Tickles."

He laughed gently, and the rush of his breath warmed her nape. For a moment they just lay there, listening to the sounds of the house settling around them. The streetlight turned the trees to black lace on the window, and outside a mockingbird trilled like a town crier announcing the "All's Well."

"I like it that they sing at night, don't you?" Evie said.

"Yeah, mockingbirds are my favorite. Tough guys."

Adam's hand rose and cupped her breast, and he sighed in contentment. Evie laid her hand on top of his and closed her eyes.

She lay quietly for a moment, content beyond her hope, and brimming with quiet expectations for good things that seemed more possible with every passing moment. She squeezed his hand, and he wrapped himself closer around her.

She found herself in a place of perfect balance. All that had gone before had fallen away, and the future held no apprehension, no fear—nothing but sweet expectations. This is what you call an embarrassment of riches, she thought.

Her heart felt full to bursting with love.

She tipped her face toward him slightly. "Thank you," she whispered.

He kissed her shoulder. "What for?"

She turned her face so that her cheek was close enough to feel his lips moving. "For this right now, for giving me this."

"My love," he said, and his words were kisses on her cheek. Then on her neck. She turned toward him, and he took her in his arms and pressed his face to her neck. "My love," he said again.

Resentment and recrimination had no hold in that perfect island of contentment; fault and blame evaporated into nothingness. Who had first left whom no longer mattered, only their hearts pressed together and the warmth and sweetness of a moment of perfect accord. They lingered together in a moment of balance, but even the sweetest moments pass and a path must be chosen. That way? Or this? A question lay be-

tween them and Evie knew the answer was hers to give.
She reached around him, resting her hands lightly on
the strong ridges of muscle that defined his back-
bone.

Every smooth curve of his body was a memory to
her. Her hands touched, remembered and explored
again the only lover she'd ever known. He hesitated
for a moment, and she knew he wasn't yet sure of what
she was offering.

She wanted to share herself with him—to be
touched, explored and remembered. But she had to
release the fear that had given her courage over the
past months. She knew the moment was passing.

"My love," she whispered into his neck.

And then he knew and understood.

Slowly at first and then with deeper understanding
and acceptance, all apprehensions turned to a mist and
evaporated. All between them was generosity, patience and tenderness. Each equally eager to give and
receive everything that love offered.

And afterward she lay replete with love in his arms,
feeling the sweet warmth of his breath rushing across
her neck and knowing that he felt just as she did. No
matter what had been said by either of them, and no
matter what doubts and fears had to be faced, they
had established an island of perfect peace and accord, and the story of their lives might possibly have
a new beginning.

Later, when love had turned to slow, sleepy ca-
resses that drift into sleep, he pulled her body close to
his and sighed. "You know," he said, "I haven't been
sleeping very well lately."

"I thought you looked tired." Her own voice sounded slow and dreamy in the quiet room.

"I think I will from now on."

"I think so, too," she said, but she was already drifting away on a misty sea of warmth and comfort, held secure by powerful arms and resting in the hope that bad times were in the past and that nothing but good things lay ahead—that the happy ending to the story of her life had been restored to her for good.

Adam heard Evie's breath become slow, then regular and even, and he felt her body relax into him as sleep overtook her.

He lay there awaiting sleep, hoping it would take him to a place of restoration and sweet oblivion. Instead, an unaccustomed vigilance descended upon him. Did I lock the patio door? he wondered. Is it time to change the batteries in the smoke detectors? Did I set the alarm?

He began to go over the things he had to accomplish tomorrow. Evie hadn't asked about his job, but when they were arguing he told her not to. And now we're both trying to be tactful, he thought. He looked at her sweet profile, made vivid by her dark hair against her pillow.

He sighed. Van Kyle had wanted him back at San Asfallia two weeks ago. He'd extended his leave beyond what was reasonable, and other men were having to handle his responsibilities. The plant needed the kind of supervision that couldn't be accomplished by telephone and fax machine, and Adam knew he would soon have to turn his responsibilities over to the man Van Kyle chose to complete his assignment.

Earlier in the week when he'd explained—in as little detail as possible—about Juliette, the old man had been generous. Well, he was as generous as someone with a multimillion-dollar investment on the line could be.

Adam squeezed his eyes, fighting the tension he felt building in his head. So much had to be done. So many people needed him. He needed to be so many places at once. But now, something new had come into his life . . . something wonderful. But changes had to be made. Life changes.

At least, he thought, I can finally get a good night's sleep. He closed his eyes and willed himself to relax.

The dreams began almost immediately.

By two o'clock he gave up trying to sleep and slipped out of bed to spend the rest of the night watching the twenty-four-hour news channel.

Chapter Ten

"Good morning," Evie said, stretching. Adam had pulled back the curtains, and the pink glow told her it was very early.

He was already dressed, and he smelled wonderful—soap and spicy cologne.

"Good morning to you," he replied, and gave her a wink from the other side of the room. He was tying his tie, and Evie watched this simple task with absorption. Over, around, under and through. She could never quite get the hang of it.

She slipped off the edge of the bed and reached for her robe. "Is our daughter awake?"

He cut a quick glance toward her in the mirror. "Yeah, she and I took an early meeting, but all's quiet on the Western Front now."

"Thank you for letting me sleep," Evie said quietly. "It's been so long since I slept so many hours at a stretch. I've been a zombie since July. You can't imagine what months of sleep deprivation makes you feel like."

He looked at her suddenly, but he didn't say anything.

"Can I make you some coffee?" she asked.

"Had some, but thanks. There's a pot on the stove."

He wore a white shirt that fell in V from his broad shoulders to his athletic hips and rounded backside. She smiled to herself. These were moments she'd always enjoyed. Almost eleven months had passed since the last time she'd watched him dress to go to the office.

When Adam prepared to go to work, he put on more than clothes; he put on his work persona. Everything about him intensified—his voice changed, and his demeanor became sharper, quick and incisive. Even his hair looked more serious.

"So," he said. "What are you doing today?"

"Major unpacking, oh, joy of joys. But then I'm going to go to the shop. I said I'd help out some—just until Olivia gets someone else. Are you hungry?"

"No, I'll get something on the way. There's not much to eat in the kitchen. Breakfast is either coffee or beer. I've been doing a lot of eating under the golden arches."

"I could offer you something of Juliette's."

"Tempting," he said, with a quick smile, "but no, thanks. I'm trying to watch my intake of baby food."

"I'll do a grocery shop then. Seems like I need to go every day."

"Mmm."

He fell quiet, and Evie assumed he was absorbed in his own thoughts. She picked at a fuzzy ball on her robe. "I'm kind of disappointed about the shop."

His gray gaze flicked her way. "Why's that?"

"Well," she said, settling on the edge of the bed, "you should have seen Something Different before I went to work there. It was okay, but it has a lot more pizzazz now." She drew her knees up and wrapped her arms around them. "Business has increased thirty percent."

His brow creased and he gave a low whistle. "Wow, that's a lot, in less than a year. We could use you at Van Kyle."

"I'll be a marketing consultant, earning thousands." Evie yawned and stretched. "Olivia says I can still use space there to sell antiques and the other, you know, things that I find."

He turned, dropped a brisk kiss on her mouth and headed for the door. "Well, I hope you find some great finds today."

"Thanks."

She jumped up and followed him down the hall. At the door he turned back as if he'd only just remembered something. "By the way, do you want to go to McGonigel's tonight? I want Rusty and Teresa to see the baby."

"Love to, who's playing?"

"It's a double bill. Shake Russell and Jack Saunders are sharing with Sisters Morales."

"Oh, honey, we'll never get in."

He grinned slyly. "I bought tickets, bar seats A and B."

"Wow, that sounds—sounds..." She frowned, not wanting to disappoint him.

"What?"

"The baby...it'll be smoky."

He looked utterly smug. "Eight o'clock. Non-smoking show."

She beamed at him. "You're a genius," she said.

"I am good, aren't I?"

She reached up and smoothed his lapels, merely for the pleasure of touching him. "I thought I'd make game hens and my famous asparagus thing for dinner."

He had leaned over to pick up his briefcase, and when her words registered he gave her a quick but appreciative smile. "That's my favorite dinner."

"I know. I'll have it ready at six-thirty so we can get to the show on time."

"Perfect. If I'm going to be thirty seconds late, I'll call."

"You'd better," she said, without rancor. She smiled and stood at the door to wave goodbye, still awash in the glow of sweet lovemaking followed by a good night's sleep.

This is going to work, she thought. We've learned some hard lessons, but now everything will be different.

Nothing will be like it was before.

She found her favorite black dress, the short one that showed off her good legs, and paid the cleaners to have it ready by four. She dashed through her day, accomplished all her shopping and still made time to add flowers and other small touches to make the house particularly pretty.

The game hens, delicate new potatoes and asparagus Evie prepared for dinner turned out to be a particular triumph that evening, and Juliette looked adorable in a pink sack and soft matching bonnet which she endured with uncharacteristic patience. By six-twenty, the candles were lit, the wine decanted, and Evie was dressed, scented and coifed for a wonderful evening.

She sat in the dining room almost giddy with anticipation of the look on Adam's face, and the delightful time they were about to enjoy together.

By seven-thirty the dinner was ruined, and at eight o'clock Evie threw it out. At eight-thirty she bathed the baby and put her to bed.

At nine she was suddenly seized with the horrifying notion that something had happened to him—that he was lying in some hospital, unable to communicate and desperate for her. The security guard at his office assured her that his car was still parked in its space and that he hadn't signed out yet. He asked Evie if she wanted him to ring through to his office.

Evie politely declined and hung up. Then she took off her dress, and at midnight she put away her book and turned off her light.

He didn't even call.

She curled up alone in the enormous bed and despised herself for believing him. She had been vulnerable.

She had been *grateful*.

She didn't cry. There was nothing to cry about anymore. Only one thought echoed in her mind.

Just like old times.

* * *

Evie woke with a start. For a moment she lay perfectly still in a moment of confusion and disorientation.

I'm back in our house.

She turned over. The pale numbers on Adam's digital alarm clock told her it was just after three. She blinked and tried to focus in the semidark. Although Adam's side of the bed wasn't rumpled, some of his clothes were strewn around the room. His jacket looked exhausted, hanging by its shoulders on the back of a chair.

Evie searched her heart for anger, but couldn't find any. All she felt was the same numbing conviction she'd felt long ago—he didn't care, he wouldn't be there, he would leave whenever it suited him.

But something inside her didn't want to believe that.

She sat up. What had woken her? she wondered. Had the baby started crying? Evie listened, but didn't hear anything. She looked at the foot of the bed for her robe, but couldn't find it. Then she remembered that earlier, when she'd been waiting up, she'd left it on the sofa in the den.

On the way down the hall, she stopped in to look at the baby. All was well in Juliette's room. The baby slept soundly, her berry red lips puckered and moving ever so slightly in her dreams of food and comfort. From his rocking chair in the corner, her bear kept solemn watch. Evie watched for a moment and then crept out.

Adam wasn't in his office. Or the den. But the curtains in front of the sliding patio doors were pulled aside, and she saw him sitting out on the deck. The moonlight had silvered his body, so he looked like a statue who'd come to life and decided to sit down on the chaise.

She tried to frown, to work up some righteous indignation, but then she saw something disturbing in the attitude of his shoulders, the way he sat and the way his head fell over into his hand. He emanated a weariness and anxiety bordering on despair.

Apprehension made her feel suddenly cold. Should I leave him alone? she wondered. No, he needs me.

When she pushed the door open, he glanced up and smiled. Then he reached his hand out for hers. "I didn't want you to wake up. You were sleeping so soundly."

When she didn't come to him, he let his hand fall. "I'm sorry, Evie."

"What happened to you?"

"I fell asleep at my desk. I woke up at twelve-thirty and figured it was too late to call."

Adam never lied, so Evie immediately accepted his words as the truth. She stepped close, and he wrapped his arm around her. "You must be very, very tired," she said.

"I was. I am." His voice sounded rough—a whisky-and-cigarettes rasp of fatigue. "Juliette woke up. I fed her and she went out again."

"You're a peach. Lucky me."

"Yeah," he said. "Lucky you."

His voice didn't match his words. Some inner conflict was tearing at him. She stood close and teased her fingers through his hair. "Why didn't you come back to bed? Not sleepy?"

"I knew I wouldn't be able to sleep," he said. Then he groaned and pulled her toward him and buried his face against her body. She touched his shoulders and felt the tension almost thrumming through him.

"What? What is it?"

He didn't answer her right away, and she tightened her arms around him. "You're scaring me, Adam."

For a long moment he didn't speak. "Evie . . ."

The sound of his torment made her suddenly very cold.

"I'm going back to San Asfallia."

I should have known. I did know.

You were stupid to believe him. He's going to leave you. Everyone leaves you. She took her hands from his body as if he burned her and almost pushed herself away.

Wait a minute, an inner voice countered, there's got to be more to it than this. She touched him again lightly and tried to keep her hands soothing. "Okay," she said, and amazed herself at the restraint in her voice. "Do you want to explain?"

His shoulders fell, but not in resignation, more as if he'd been unburdened. "Sit down for a minute?"

The chaise was wide and armless, so she sat down beside him. The light from the moon was bright enough for her to see his face clearly, though she knew her own was in shadow. She was glad of that. "Okay," she said. "I'm sitting."

For a moment he didn't speak. Obviously gathering his words, she thought. With a sinking heart she wondered how bad this was going to be.

This is where I start saying goodbye again.

He looks beautiful, she thought, striking and supernatural. The full moon had turned his body to the color of mercury.

"You were right all along about me. About the way I'd feel about having children."

Evie felt herself go cold and still. "What are you saying?" Her voice was rising. "Are you saying you don't want—?"

"Wait a minute," he said. "Let me finish." He took a weary breath. "When I talked to Van Kyle last week, I told him I couldn't finish the assignment. He was disappointed, and he also told me he'd already picked out my next posting. A project in Egypt. Four years. It sounded like my fantasy come true. Exciting work, exotic place—you know. But of course he couldn't give it to me because of the baby, and for a minute, well . . ." he hesitated.

"My first thought was I wish we'd waited." He shook his head. "And then I thought, my God, Evie was right. What kind of man am I? She was right all along. If it were left up to me we'd never settle down and have a family like we'd planned. I would drag her all around the world, I'd have my work and my pretty wife, and that's as far as I thought."

Evie felt her throat closing. "And then?"

"And then I thought about Juliette. Evie, I can't tell you how I feel about that little girl. My head hurts it's so full. And I'm scared, too. Am I going to be a good father? Can I protect her from the things that happened to me?"

"I think all parents worry about that," Evie said. "Everyone who has children worries about those things."

He sighed heavily. "I know. But, anyway, I was sitting there in my office getting ready to come home, and that's when I decided, I have to go back to San Asfallia. I won't be gone for long."

"Oh," she said. "That's nice."

How odd, she thought, I don't feel a thing.

"Please don't pull away from me, Evie."

"I'm not going anywhere."

"Yes, you are. I can feel it."

"I don't mean to."

He leaned forward and took her hand. He kissed her palm, then wound his fingers through hers and pressed her hand to his chest. His heart was pounding.

"You see, I've been having these horrible dreams. Well, at least I thought they were horrible, but now I know—I understand what's going on."

"Dreams?" she said. *God, I hate the way my voice sounds.* "What dreams?"

He told her everything—the screaming of the locomotive and the baby crying.

"That is horrible."

"Now I don't think so. I'm beginning to think it's the deepest part of me—the soul inside me telling me when I'm losing a part of myself. The train dreams came back in South America because I was losing you. And the child crying—well, you know what I almost lost."

"That's so strange," Evie murmured. "It's like part of you knew she was yours."

"I know." He squeezed her hand. "I think so, too. We're connected, Evie. You and me and Juliette. I can't explain what you and I have together, but there's something I do know. Remember when you told me years ago, when you first met me, that you knew that I was going to be part of your life story? Well, I felt the same way, but not until the day I kissed you in the Alexanders' kitchen. Until that moment I didn't really see you, but after that there's never been a moment that you aren't in my mind.

He squeezed her hand again. "But that first minute was like someone took a blindfold off me, and there you were—the love of my life.

"And with Juliette, well, this gets spooky, but I think part of me knew you were pregnant that Christmas. And then, when you said you were adopting a baby, that awareness just came to life."

He turned away, and his face in profile was solemn and thoughtful, like an image on a coin. "I love you two more than I ever thought possible. I thought I would love my children, but I never expected to feel this way. It scares me and it makes me wonder how well I know myself."

She teased his knee up and rested her chin on top of it. "So why are you leaving us?"

"I started having dreams again. Right away. Last night. I was back in Marline, standing by the tracks holding a berry picking can, and then a train came. When the caboose passed by I saw a man standing outside at the safety rail. He didn't wave he just stood there—empty looking—and I looked in his face, and it was me."

Gooseflesh rose on Evie's arms. "That's horrible."

He turned back toward her. "I don't think so. I think that was a kind of warning.

"You see, Evie, there's a big part of me that has to do with my work, with who I am as a breadwinner and a man. It's the kind of man I am and I can't change. I don't even know if I want to. I'll always need challenging work. I can't sit at a desk in downtown Houston and push a pencil. I'd go nuts. I have to do work in the field.

"I like working with men like my father. Roughnecks, roustabouts—all those hardworking simple guys are part of who I am. Working with them makes me feel alive. If I didn't do my work, I'd lose part of myself."

"So," Evie asked woodenly, "How many times a year do you think you'll come home?" You're going to miss so much, you stupid man, she thought. The things I thought I had taken from you, you're going to throw away.

He reached up and grabbed her shoulders. "You make me nuts."

She didn't look up at him. "Just answer the question."

"Well," he said quietly. "There are fifty-two weeks in a year. Every year I guess I'll be gone for about ten weeks—fifteen at the most—altogether. Let's see, fifty-two minus ten equals—"

"What? What do you mean ten weeks? The assignments last for months—years."

He laughed. "Well, I won't be taking the long-term assignments anymore, sweetheart. But I do want to do fieldwork. As much as I'd like to come home every single night and play pat-a-cake with our little girl and play footsie with you, I belong in the field. I'm a great negotiator. I get along well with the men. I'm great with languages and—"

She put her hand over his mouth. "You're a conceited windbag."

He pulled her hand away, kissed her fingers and lightly bit her wrist. "Ah, sweetheart, you turn a man's head with the things you say."

"So that's it? Ten or fifteen weeks a year?"

"That's it. The longest it'll be is three weeks at a time, maybe a month."

"You're sure?"

"Positive."

"And the rest of the time? Will you come home when you say you will?"

"How about if I promise to call?"

She dug her nails lightly into his leg.

"Ow!"

"You better," she said. "If you don't I'll give your credit cards to our daughter and drop her off at the Galleria."

Adam's laugh faded to seriousness. "So this sounds good to you?"

"Actually, I couldn't have planned it better myself."

"You don't mind my being gone? I mean, it is two to three months a year, when you add it up."

"Darling," she said. "I adore you, but these are busy years for me, too. I'm a mother, now. And, you know, I miss my friends in Evansville. When you're out, I'll go see the Alexanders." Her voice fell. "And I suppose I'll need to make peace with Uncle Richard. And there's the shop, too. Olivia's the businesswoman, but I'm the artist." She sighed. "I think our being apart might turn out to have been a good thing. I learned some things about myself that I didn't know before. The things I missed and didn't miss surprised me. I was so lonesome for my garden, I couldn't stand it, and then I figured out one of the things I liked most about it."

"What's that?"

"The neatness, the order. All the safety of having the plants completely safe and controlled in their little beds." She laughed a little. "Having Juliette made me less uptight about those things, and at the same time I found out I got some real satisfaction out of working. So you see," she said, "you're not the only one who has the things to do and places to go. Actually, you'll be lucky if I have time for you when you're in town."

The laughter between them was light, not the laughter of humor, but of two people trying to establish a contact that had been broken. Evie knew they were again reaching tentatively for each other, trying to establish a new life without losing the magic of the one they'd shared before.

Adam grew suddenly still. "We've got a lot to work on."

"I know," she said. "Lucky for us we're young. Well, at least I am."

He grabbed at her playfully, and she blocked his hands with her own.

Then he took a deep breath, looked at her for a moment and pulled her down on the chaise beside him. The kiss was warm and lingering.

His mouth was slightly salty, but she could still taste the brandy he'd had earlier. He touched her face, tangled his hands in her hair and with a simple motion he was on top of her.

"You're crying," he murmured, kissing the silver tears on her cheeks.

"Am I? That's strange. I'm happy. I'm happier than I ever thought I could be."

Her hands moved up his powerful flanks, and her fingers dusted across his ribs, the flat planes of his chest, up to his collarbones and behind his neck. Her hands looked pale against his dark skin.

"You're beautiful in this light," he said. "Your hair around your face—it looks—" He sighed. "I don't have the words."

"Kiss me then," she said. "Tell me that way."

Slowly he lowered himself to her, and her heart accelerated at the feel of his weight and warmth pressing down and covering her. She curved her legs around him, urging him to join with her.

She gave him all her tenderness, all her passion and all her trust. "I love you, Adam."

And in return he gave her his strength, his desire and his deepest self made whole at last. "I'll always love you, Evangeline."

And they both knew there would always be enough for each other, and for their children, and for their children's children.

There would be plenty, plenty to go around.

*   *   *   *   *

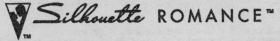

Take 4 bestselling love stories FREE

Plus get a FREE surprise gift!

As seen on TV!
Free Gift Offer

With a Free Gift proof-of-purchase from any Silhouette® book,
you can receive a beautiful cubic zirconia pendant.

This gorgeous marquise-shaped stone is a genuine cubic
zirconia—accented by an 18" gold tone necklace.

(Approximate retail value $19.95)

Send for yours today...
compliments of ▼ *Silhouette*®
™

To receive your free gift, a cubic zirconia pendant, send us one original proof-of-
purchase, photocopies not accepted, from the back of any Silhouette Romance™,
Silhouette Desire®, Silhouette Special Edition®, Silhouette Intimate Moments®
or Silhouette Yours Truly™ title available in August, September or October at your favorite
retail outlet, together with the Free Gift Certificate, plus a check or money order for
$1.65 u.s./$2.15 can. (do not send cash) to cover postage and handling, payable
to Silhouette Free Gift Offer. We will send you the specified gift. Allow 6 to 8 weeks for
delivery. Offer good until October 31, 1996 or while quantities last. Offer valid in the
U.S. and Canada only.

Free Gift Certificate

Name: _____

Address: _____

City: _____ State/Province: _____ Zip/Postal Code: _____

Mail this certificate, one proof-of-purchase and a check or money order for postage
and handling to: SILHOUETTE FREE GIFT OFFER 1996. In the U.S.: 3010 Walden
Avenue, P.O. Box 9077, Buffalo NY 14269-9077. In Canada: P.O. Box 613, Fort Erie,
Ontario L2Z 5X3.

FREE GIFT OFFER   084-KMD
ONE PROOF-OF-PURCHASE
To collect your fabulous FREE GIFT, a cubic zirconia pendant, you must include this
original proof-of-purchase for each gift with the properly completed Free Gift Certificate.

084-KMD

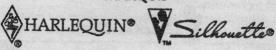